Raves for the W of JOYCE C~~~~~~~~~~~~~

"Few writers better illuminate the mind's most disturbing corners."
—*Seattle Times*

"Oates is a mind-reader who writes psychological horror stories about seriously disturbed minds, and it's hard to tear your eyes away."
—*New York Times Book Review*

"I love her writing…Oates is simply the most consistently inventive, brilliant, curious, and creative writer going, as far as I'm concerned."
—*Gillian Flynn, author of GONE GIRL*

"Wrenching…a grim examination of how humans cope with unspeakable physical and psychological pain. She illuminates the darkest corners and shows us the startled, troubled creatures hiding there, nursing their wounds, staring back at us, their kin."
—*Cleveland Plain Dealer*

"Dread, in fiction, can be a magnificent thing…Oates isn't writing horror fiction, but she might as well be. Her stories pack the same kind of visceral wallop."
—*Los Angeles Times*

"Brilliant…A shattered spirit, furious, violent, confused, a creature of the gothic underbelly where Oates's sympathies most often lie…breathtaking."
—*Washington Post*

"Grimly compelling…terrifyingly hallucinatory."
—*Wall Street Journal*

"Sinister, edgy, delectably creepy."
—*San Francisco Chronicle*

"A graceful and excruciating story."
—*USA Today*

"Powerful…feverish."
—*The New Yorker*

"Immensely moving."
—*People*

"Seethes with Oates' trademark intellect and psychological insight…delivers nightmares that are…unforgettable."
—*Elle*

"An urgently compelling and drastically revealing study of evil, habitual terror, and survival."
—*Booklist*

"Rarely is [Oates] so intriguing as when she strays into a genre best described as 'faction.' It's as unsettling as it is worthwhile to take a fresh look at a much-publicized event or personality through Oates' eyes."
—*Times (London)*

"Joyce Carol Oates explores in fiction what most of us only experienced through headlines some twenty-five years ago."
—*Henry Louis Gates, Jr.*

I didn't have my guitar any longer. I did have the Machete with me, which I usually carried wound in many yards of coarse woven cloth some girl gave me, brought back from Taos, to go with my primitive good looks, but where was the Machete...?

The dressmaker's dummy with all the blood was lying on it. The handle was showing. Weird-red, glowing-red, pink-scarlet-sinister radiance. It glowed in the dark. I crawled over to her and said, "Honey you didn't tell me your name, even," and it wasn't until later that day when I had escaped and was having a tamale-burger at a Strip drive-in, standing near some teenage bastard and his bright yellow Ferrari with the radio blaring, that I heard the news bulletin, but by then...by then the memory of it had all evaporated and I felt only that fuzzy little interest, you know, that you feel when you hear about four or five stewardesses murdered in some bungalow they rented out in Pasadena that the neighbors swore had been raided three times in the last three months for drugs and wild parties and late-night noises so I had only a foggy good citizen's interest in that, because my real self was with my music but my music was shut off and all those powers that went with it that I lost in the scramble-climb up Vanbrugh's house while those bastards stood around clapping and cheering and snickering...

The TRIUMPH of the SPIDER MONKEY

by Joyce Carol Oates

A HARD CASE CRIME NOVEL

A HARD CASE CRIME BOOK
(HCC-140)
First Hard Case Crime edition: July 2019

Published by

Titan Books
A division of Titan Publishing Group Ltd
144 Southwark Street
London SE1 0UP

in collaboration with Winterfall LLC

Print edition ISBN 978-1-78565-677-4
E-book ISBN 978-1-78565-772-6

Design direction by Max Phillips
www.signalfoundry.com

Typeset by Swordsmith Productions

The name "Hard Case Crime" and the Hard Case Crime logo are trademarks of Winterfall LLC. Hard Case Crime books are selected and edited by Charles Ardai.

Printed in the United States of America

Visit us on the web at www.HardCaseCrime.com

—for those on the Outside

slowly we are overrunning the earth
spidermonkeys twittering climbing leaping leering
on broken banjos

the Jukebox of the 40's could not cage us in
stunned, the arm of the mechanism pauses
paralyzed

when the Spider Monkeys inside
open soul-doors to us spidermonkeys skinned alive
the magic of My Passage on Earth
will be just another headline

THE TRIUMPH OF THE SPIDER MONKEY

I
Nativity

Noise, vibrations, murmuring nosey crowd of bastards with nothing else to do but gawk—grunting sweating bastard in a uniform reaching in and grabbing me out of the darkness and delivering me to light—

—to lights, that is—

Holding me up to those lights. *A baby! A baby still alive!*

Time: 6:05 PM. Date: February 14, 1944.

Delivered by the Master Key endowed by its creator to open all the lockers, foot-lockers renting for 25c for 24 hours—delivered by some amazed outraged bastard in a uniform to the surprise and anger and gradual disappointment of the crowd *(It's still alive…a baby, yeh, locked in there…but it's still alive…Yeh. Let's go.)* Held up to the lights and declared *Still alive* in the Trailways Bus Terminal on Canal Street, New York City, New York, as good a place as any. The time had been 5:55 PM when the disturbance began. The Master Key was summoned, and delivered out of its duffel bag the screaming ungrateful little—

"Bobbie Gotteson" hears the name "Bobbie Gotteson" uttered and a long loud string of words he tries to interrupt, rising to his feet though his legs are weak, interrupting the words to cry "I Bobbie Gotteson being of sound mind and body do hereby request—insist—want—" while the Judge stares and the courtroom goes wild and the bailiffs and the police converge—and the Maniac falls back in his chair— Counsel is advised by someone very angry to instruct his client "Bobbie Gotteson" to refrain from such outbursts this is a Court of Law he is on trial for his life if that can't make him into a sober mature responsible adult what will?*

—screaming ungrateful little red-faced monkeyish diaper-soaked Bobbie Gotteson, delivered to the gawkers out of footlocker 79-C, already in trouble with the Law. Mouthy little sonuvabitch. Mouth runs away with it though on trial for its life, just as mouth ran away with it at the age of 1 week. Mouth has a sense of humor. Jokes too much. Gets the rest of it into trouble, as the Prosecuting Attorney is going to show in all that detail, the bastard. Public records will show and are never wrong. Public records were following closely and were never wrong causing taxpayers to rebel...*What, is it still alive?... Alive?* Bobbie

*One of Gotteson's fixed ideas was that he faced death in the gas chamber, though he had been told repeatedly that capital punishment had been abolished in the State of California. All remarks in this strange document are the Maniac's even those he attributes to the "court" and to other people.

Gotteson is already there, existing in the typed-up words in the reports and can't be erased or wished away by the friendliest Friends of the Court or the pickets (mainly kids, looking skinnier and uglier and crazier than I do) outside this Hall of Justice, picketing for the release of the Maniac. Mouth might as well confess. Mouth might as well inform on itself.

When the screaming stopped and the diapers were changed the joking started, but jokes only got it into trouble. You wouldn't think so, but it was true. Into trouble and into it deeper and deeper, a total of seventeen years four months fourteen days spent Inside, but with a cheerful natural bright sense of humor and a basic optimism that ebbed or was kicked hard occasionally but always surfaced again. Sheer delight is the Maniac's energy, always bubbling back, the best trick of all as was demonstrated on Variety Night or Talent Show nights, and afterward in the Outside World (which you inhabit not knowing it is Outside of other people's Inside, but more of that later!—later!), but somehow sweetest of all when fellow inmates doubled over with laughter and sometimes had to beg it to stop, *Jesus Bobbie, Jesus kid, cut it out you're killing me*—! What did they like best? Popular opinion divided equally between the *spider-monkey-climbing-up-a-pole* routine and the *spastic-crossing-the-freeway* pantomine. Inmates showed surprising enthusiasm and spontaneous interest in these amateur nights—even the most hardened criminals, even the crudest and hardest of heart could find a tear, or laugh till tears rolled down their coarse cheeks…which only goes to show you…doesn't it?…But wouldn't you know it, no surprise, that's human nature, after the first flush of excitement and enthusiasm interest in Variety Night or Talent Show Night always faded away, and the hard work, the hard grinding work, had to be done by just a core of prisoners…you can't beat human nature, Inside or Out. Hard work to organize rehearsals and paint scenery and fight people off and find a lonely corner somewhere to practice your songs and dance-routines and mimes, so by the time *And now—little Bobbie Gotteson!* summons you out of the wings and onstage you are haggard and weary and must pull yourself up by your own gray wool-and-cotton socks, so to speak, in an effort to appear happy. But I had a natural talent for show business, for pleasing the crowd, I was always singled out for applause and encouraged to express myself by people in uniforms, so as to induce paroxysms of laughter in other people, or maybe a stray tear.

If it please Your Honor and the Ladies and Gentlemen of the Jury my client is quieted down and people can stop snickering and gawking and prodding one another and giggling in the corners…and that motherfucker on the bench can stop smirking and trying to catch Bobbie's moist brown eye with a wink…and the fact remains as a matter of Public Record that the Maniac was delivered to the world out of Locker 79-C in the main waiting room of the Trailways Bus Terminal on Canal Street New York City, as good a place as any and why are you snickering?—the dark, dark odorous Inside of the locker and the urine-soaked duffel bag were sweet to our Bobbie, as to anyone on the other side of sanity.

2
The Maniac Explains His Sanity

I can play sane, like you. Like everyone. Sometimes I played insane, but now I am very sane. My mind is a net, with holes in it that can be very tiny or quite large; to sift things through or to catch them.

Twice my life was saved by playing insane. The first time, in a jail in Reno on my way out here, I woke up and some old wire-bearded bastard was staring down into my face. His lips were moving. He seemed to see me inside, his eyes were really scooping into mine, and he started mumbling some words about his *little girl*. He grabbed hold of me and tried to embrace me. He said I had a little girl's mouth, that it was *his* little girl, a terrible panic ran everywhere in me and I began to beat him around the face to make him let go of me, but he wouldn't let go, he was shrieking now, and I butted at his face with the top of my head, in a rage, to make him let go of me. *My little girl! My girl!* Like hell I am your little girl, Gotteson raged, Gotteson with his muscles and his chest-hair and his deep bass voice, but when he fell down and grabbed my legs I saw he was hurt bad, there would be trouble, already the sheriff's men were headed for us, so I proceeded to go crazy. It saved me from a beating. I was transferred to a psychiatric ward in a hospital that was very modern, and after a while charges were dropped against me, whatever they were, maybe loitering or vagrancy. I was always an expert actor. At another place where they give you tokens for behaving well, instead of beating you, I acted so well that I accumulated heavy sagging pockets filled with tokens.

Another time my life was saved by playing insane, out here. A contact came to pick me up, in a blue Ferrari, and he told me to leave behind my guitar because it wouldn't be needed tonight. I asked him what was wrong. I asked if the client had changed his mind, if the party was called off, and he said well, no, the client has not changed his mind but the instructions were different from what I had been told. He said to put on a blindfold he had in the glove compartment. So I put it on. But I took the guitar with me because there wasn't a safe place to leave it, and we drove out somewhere up into the Hills, that was pretty obvious, and I just relaxed and thought well hell, I would just relax and not even make nervous jokes to the man who was driving, but try to sit calmly, and relax. So we stopped somewhere out in the country. He said, O.K., take the blindfold off, it's already past ten and we were due at ten, so we got out and he opened the trunk of the car and took out two leather thongs with fringes on them and a leather arm-band with something propped up on it. I asked him what the hell that was, but he said just to put it on, so I buckled it on my forearm and a car came around a curve just then, so in the headlights I saw that it was a bird pasted onto the arm-band, and it was so strange with its glass eyes and sharp curved beak that I stood staring at it while the car went by, and my friend shouted at me to wake up, or we'd both be in trouble. He had put on a helmet with a feathery fringe to it, going all around the helmet though longer at the sides and the back, and he told me to get going up through the brush and began to explain what the assignment was. We would be told to stop, he said, but we must not even pause—must shout *No mercy! No mercy!*— and keep on beating the client. I began to concentrate my powers inside my head. By the time we smashed our way through a terrace door and into the sunken living room where a man sat watching television I was all on fire and could not have been stopped except by bullets. The stuffed falcon shivered on my arm. The client, seeing my face, began to scream. But there was no stopping me and *no mercy*.

In a frenzy I slashed at the client's bare exposed face and could not hear what people were shouting. A kind of blackness came over me. I seemed to fall through the floor, as if the thick white woolly carpeting of that expensive home vanished and there were coarse floorboards with cracks between them and boards missing in places, through which I fell in my excitement. On all sides I danced and lunged. I was wiry, wily. I was galvanized with energy as if energy shot through me in spasms....And then I was being dragged somewhere, then someone was shouting at me that it was a mistake, we had broken into the wrong house, and I must stop what I was doing. Must stop! Gotteson need never stop, I told him. Why should Gotteson stop once he begins? It is all inertia, a vast mountain slow to begin its upheaval and then hungry to continue, in fact unstoppable. Gotteson showed *no mercy.*

And so I pretended madness, to save myself from disaster. Yet I was always sane. I am like you: a progression of states of mind, forms of sanity that keep moving and eluding definition. I was always sane and had practiced insanity so well that in falling through the floorboards I came upon an earlier wiser self, that seemed to know the way out of that house and had no need for the shouting of my friend. Outside, on the terrace, I was overcome by a flash of certainty, a forward-leaping vision of what I must do—what I had already done, in the future, and only needed to remember now in detail—and I wound the leather thong around my friend's neck in order to strangle him into collapsing, not into absolute death, and so escape. All this was done with calculation, though it took place in two or three minutes—rushed and frenzied and noisy—and I ran back down the hill through the underbrush to safety.

A Maniac is immortal. He cannot be killed except by his own manipulations.

THE COURTSHIP OF THE SPIDER MONKEY

there she is awaiting him
alone in a hole
that is a room
in a house honeycombed
with holes

hand-over-hand he climbs
foot-over-foot up the side of the house
the master of gravity
concentrated as a bridegroom

the Moon and the Machete
communicate with winks

The courtroom is restless. The third juror from the left, in the back row, is staring at the Maniac with a look glistening as the Maniac's. There is something about the Machete that excites us all.

3
The Machete

It sliced up more people than they have records for, how's that for a tease? You think that the State's records show everything?—every slash? There were more brides than I remember. The Machete was, is, two and a half feet long, purchased at an Army–Navy Surplus Store in town here, a blade of steel, a sturdy man-sized handle, nothing like that thing the Prosecution has under its control. *That* blade is dull. If it is stained, the stains are rust and not blood. You can't bring the Spider Monkey's powers into the Hall of Justice; you can't even see the Machete except by moon-light

Doreen B. waited like a tender space to be threaded, the way you thread a needle. I didn't know her name until the next day, until the newspapers came out.

4
Gotteson's Juvenilia

Poems written at the age of 15, about which
his English teacher at the Vocational High School
in Newark, New Jersey, said "These are
the products of a sick mind, Bobbie."

THE TRAIN
a toy train the size of a real train
was stalled in the dark in a field
the temperature on both sides of the glass was 0°
but the passengers were shouting anyway
    to get out
they were pounding on the windows
so I drove out with a fireman's ax
to smash the windows and let them loose
but the ax got away from me and flew through
    the dark
and when it returned to me it was bloody
and there were hairs on it

this taught me to be patient
and wait in the dark

THE COCOON

I was sleeping in the cocoon
stretched out to the exact size of the cocoon
five foot seven and a half inches
I was sleeping there and very happy
then the alarm rang
my foster-brothers ran into the room
my foster-father grabbed me by the ankles
I screamed for him not to pull me down
    backwards
but he laughed and said "Time to get up!"
they all laughed and dragged me backwards
out of the cocoon

when you are yanked backwards like that
the insides of the cocoon turn to razors
even your eyes are pressed into your head
by the time your head is free
your brain is suffocated
but you get dressed anyway
and go to school anyway
hoping no one will notice

THE FOOD-CHAIN BLUES

when you are inside the package
you can't read the insignia on front
or the magic Date of Expiration
past which you will turn
unhygienic

5
Unrehearsed Interview
With a Child Therapist, Somewhere in Newark

THERAPIST

…your mother has issued a complaint, says she had to call the police on you, Bobbie. For shame! What's your explanation this time? Why do you make life so hard for yourself and your family and this office?

BOBBIE

…not my family. They're not my family.

THERAPIST

Your father isn't well, it says here. Kidney ailment, eh? Your mother has issued a formal complaint saying that she's at the end of *her rope*, her exact words; she can't handle you and her own children—says all three of you are uncontrollable—

BOBBIE

They promised not to go after me. They said so. I told them I could protect myself.…said I'd take them both with me. I could do it.—It wasn't my father; it was my foster-father. It wasn't kidneys that killed him. Somebody backed over him in a—

THERAPIST

...Looking through your files is quite a revelation. Quite a revelation!...Did poorly on the Wenshler Verbal Skills when you were six...I.Q. somewhere between 48 and 78...Hardison–Radt Abstraction–Perception very, very poor...Faulty development of conceptualizing abilities... plus disjointed motor coordination and speech mannerisms....What's that sniffling? Are you sniffling?

BOBBIE

No. Not me.

THERAPIST

It's obvious that you need love, obvious as the funny pug nose on your face, eh-heh, but *who* has got the stomach for it...the crucial question of our era. Eh? The last time I fell for that sniffling trick, my boy, and put my hand out to one of you—a cute little creature with cartoon freckles and big brown weepy eyes—the little bastard bit my finger down to the bone, bit right through the joint and swallowed the fingertip, nail and all. Here, look at this. How I screamed! What agony!—And for *what?* What was accomplished? They offered to stomach-pump my fingertip out of him and graft it back on me, but *no thanks!* I didn't even want it back after that disgusting experience ....how to continue as a professional with integrity, a complex multi-dimensional young man with high ideals, confronted hourly by meager one-dimensional stereotypes like you....I want subtlety, is it too much to ask?...Your father's dead, you say? Did you say he's dead?

BOBBIE

It wasn't my father.

THERAPIST

That reminds me, Bobbie, the law requires that you be placed at all times in a home with both parents living—with both a mother and a father. So I'm afraid we'll have to move you.

BOBBIE

I'm ready to go.

THERAPIST

It will only take a few weeks to get the papers cleared, and in the meanwhile I can have one of the secretaries type up these forms....Why are you squirming like that? Don't you feel well?

BOBBIE

I'm ready to go. Wherever you people send me. I can pick up and go anywhere. I'm ready. I'm ready all the time—night or day. I don't sleep. I stay awake so I can be ready.

THERAPIST

That's fascinating, Bobbie. And you're only—how old?—this record says you're fourteen, but you look older to me. You look a lot older to me. You're about the hairiest monkey-ugly fourteen-year-old bastard I've seen in a long time, Bobbie. It's pathetic, actually. I think what we'll do is, to take a few short-cuts, just telephone juvenile court and set up a date, and that way your mother can dump you without a lot of red tape. Back you go into the bin! Back for the tax-payers to feed! Yes, it's the same old story. Your original mother dumped you, and the State took you on. Fed you, changed your diapers, educated you, set you up in excellent foster homes, but you can't appreciate it, can you?—with your monkey-ugly little face, that certainly looks as if it needs a shave. Is that the beginning of a beard...? It's obscene, actually, to sit knee-to-knee with a creature like you. You're not human. You don't appreciate what people do for you. Huge taxes go into public education, yet kids like you roam the streets illiterate; you can barely read the street signs and can manage to tell one brand-name of automobile from another only by counting the number of letters....

BOBBIE

I'm ready to go...I can go to the next place from here...I can walk to it....I've defeated the force of gravity....I can go anywhere.

THERAPIST

Uh, yes. It's obvious to our office that you're going to grow up as an institutionalized person, and from the looks of you you'll be involved in a murder in a few years—from the looks of your shoulders and arm muscles *you'll* probably do the strangling, though it could be the other way around if you cross up your sweetheart and he gets angry at you. But I could be mistaken: you could grow up on the Outside. In which case I'm sure you *will* do the murdering yourself. But you won't make a penny out of it. The royalties will go to complete strangers. The starring role in the movie will go—of course—to someone handsomer than you, and of course much taller. You're just too short to be taken seriously. No, you won't make a penny out of it, you'll be famous but back in the bin again, eating out of the tax-payers' hand forever. That's the way it is with little monkey-bastards like you, you just lose. Right? It's a losing game. You can't win....But there's no point in crying about it, or whatever you're doing. That wheezing noise won't change the constitution of the universe, Bobbie. Forget it. I'll get you back in Boys' Home right in the city here and you'll be off the streets and safe for a while from your own evil nature. Will you please stop crying? Don't you have a Kleenex? It's disgusting, actually, to have to witness behavior like yours...a man like myself begins with high ideals, goes into graduate school prepared to devote himself to humanity, and what does he end up sitting knee-to-knee with?—little blue-chinned muscle-bound monkey-faced bastards like Bobbie Gadsen...or Gotsen...or Gotteson, whatever the hell this word is, the typist X'd half the word out. *You're a word that's been half-X'd out, Bobbie!* Poor little bastard!

6
El Portal
The First Night

"I'll just pretend you're not here," she said.

"What should I do?" I said.

She walked away. She turned her back to me. I could see the spine beneath the skin, rippling there, the vertebrae moving like tiny knuckles...and the front of her face was slit sideways with a grin, I knew it though I couldn't see it.

"What should I do?" I shouted.

She laughed and walked away. She walked across the terrace. The wind got into her fluffy pale hair and she clutched at it with both hands, helplessly. She turned her body so that the wind moved with it, eased along it. She was laughing. I stared at her and knew what I was expected to do. They were expecting me to do it. She jumped up on the wall—it was a narrow wall made of rock—and walked along on top of it, her arms outstretched as if she were sleepwalking, balancing herself above that fifteen hundred foot drop. She glanced back at me, her eyes narrowed in excitement. The sun was behind a thin tissue of clouds. A rainbow formed and dissolved. She was laughing, her porcelain-white teeth were laughing at me, she cried over her shoulder, "You little monkey!—hairy little honey-monkey!" This made me laugh, against my will. They were watching. They were expecting me to do something. So I ran across the terrace and followed along beside her, while she pranced above me, darting these little mock-loving glances at me, drawing her lips together in a shocked pout, then smiling, then grinning, while behind her things were sailing in the air—circling—constantly circling and looking for food—"Watch out for the buzzards, they might get in your hair," I said. She giggled. I didn't touch her, just to tease her. "They might get in your hair like bats and snarl you all up, tear into you, they might poke out your eyes and that wouldn't be so funny, would it?" I cried. From this angle I could see the thickening flesh around her jaw, she wasn't as young as I had thought, and the flesh of her upper arms was loose, very pale, wobbly, strange....."You should wear more clothes," I said. "You should cover yourself up more. Except your legs, your legs are all right...your legs are very nice." She couldn't hear me because of the wind, she paused and cupped her hand to her ear. "Your legs are very nice!" I shouted.

"Louder!" she said, waving over my head. I supposed there was a camera and a sound-track machine behind me. How close were they?— would they use a zoom lens? I danced along beside her, beginning to snatch at her, just picking at her as if I were picking feathers—little pinches of my thumb and forefinger—pinching her thighs, her legs while she giggled and hopped away from me. One of the hawks darted down straight into the water behind us. She screamed, surprised. She jumped down from the wall and into my arms. We staggered backward, laughing. I began to tear at her clothing. It was all open in the back, scooped down to below her waist, and I tore it into pieces while she screamed and tried to get her fingers around my throat. "No you don't, no you don't!" I said.

"I'm not one of your little-girl sluts!" she screamed. "I'm famous! I don't need you! I don't need to be humiliated like this!—Stop that, you little bastard, I'll have you arrested—stop that!— I said stop that!"

"Your face is slipping to one side," I whispered. "Your mascara is running—"

But she was scratching at me and didn't hear. "Little wop bastard! Little monkey-bastard!"

"I'm not a wop," I said. "I'm an American.—Don't you care, your make-up is all slipping down?"

We wrestled together on the flagstone terrace. She shrieked and tried to roll away from me. I straddled her. "I have a son your age, stop this, I have a son—I have two sons—I don't need you to do this—I'm above this—I—I'll have you put on Death Row!—stop it!—you're diseased, you're sub-human, stop it, my children are here—they're watching—I know they're loose and watching—stop—wait—" I put my hand over her mouth, the gritty dirty palm of my right hand. She tried to wrench away. How we laughed together, secretly!—behind my hand, how we laughed! And the universe grew powerful, every cell of my body leaped with the desire *to do well*, and I—

She got loose and waved wildly back at the house, where they were standing and applauding. She jumped to her feet, but I grabbed hold of her leg at the calf, then at the thigh, and yanked her down again. "Stop him, I'm sick, I'm raw, I'm worn out!" she cried, but they ignored her screams; only the cameraman approached us, barefoot, crooning words that seemed to be addressed to me. I didn't pay attention to them. Found a clump of her blond hair in my fist. "Oh Bobbie, Bobbie, Bobbie you maniac," someone crooned. It might have been the cameraman. It might have been Melva.

Afterward sometime I lay at the shallow end of the pool, utterly still. The pores of my body were now closed. I could hear them inside the house. I thought, *I will close myself from them.* But one eye remained open, sharply, slyly, focussing on Bobbie Gotteson now on film, one of his performances now on film, one of his performances on film at last, though it wasn't the performance Bobbie had hoped to give. But...!

Oh Bobbie, Bobbie, Bobbie you handsome monkey, you sweet maniac, oh Bobbie, where did you come from? — what powers do you possess?

7

The Maniac Meditates
Upon His Powers and When They First
Got Him into Trouble

I heard somebody yelling at her in my own voice—it was a boy yelling—a boy maybe eleven or twelve years old—yelling—

Didn't she know, the nasty stinky ugly old bitch, that I could set fire to this place if I wanted to?—could set fire to the stinky place we lived in and the stinky living room sofa where I had to sleep and the stairs and the whole building—didn't she know this simple fact? Didn't she know that I could set fire to her too and she'd go up in smoke, her baggy dresses and her underskirts and underwear all flaming up in smoke, didn't she know—?

Which one of them was this?

One of them, I don't know which one; one of my mothers.

Yes, just listen: I yelled at her (it was some woman grabbing me by the shoulders tough and ready to bite and screaming back into my face) and when that didn't work I whispered starting to sob, didn't she know that I could do anything if I let my mind free?—if I unleashed it to do my secret will? And she just shook me and screamed and banged me against the wall and the radiator and my powers rushed to me, filling out my skinny arms and legs and chest, but she had more power, she had the power of thumping me back against the radiator so my left leg was in terrible pain and I could not get my mind razor-sharp enough to slice sideways through her. "…could light fire to you and you'd go up…" but nobody gave a damn, but right at that instant the melody of a song shot through my mind…and much, much later…much later…five or six years later…fooling around with a guitar in the Recreation Unit…the melody and the complete lyrics of my first song came to me, complete. Do you know it? Does anybody know it? They stole it and changed the words but the words are *Could set fire! to you! and you'd go up!* and no other words.…

I wrote a hundred songs, two hundred, a thousand!… People here don't believe me, they hate me. But pals of mine back in the East or out here, and Inside, *they* would not lie…would not try to cheat me…*they* would vouch for me! That song on the back of the Survivors' hit single, a few months ago, the one they called "Learning to Love"— that's *my* song—you check out the record and see, it's my name down there, *Bobbie Gotteson* right there in the credits.…But the bastards cheated me. They cheated me like everybody else cheated me. They took my song and changed the title to that shitty title—*my* song was called "Unlearning to Live" and was a beautiful song—and those bastards, always screwing around and zonked out of their heads half the time, millionaire-bastards, *my own age!*—

they bought my song from me for twelve lousy hundred dollars and changed the title and the words and— Melva's son, the bastard is *younger than I am!*—the bastard heard me singing at Lucky Pierre's, that's on the Strip, and hung around and told me how good I was, and—

Then they got an injunction with the police. They tried to defraud me. They tried to curtail my rights as a citizen. I was born in this country like everyone else! *I am an American through and through!* And they got a Jew lawyer to defraud me of my rights, got the Los Angeles Police Department to come move me out of that house—where I was an invited guest—where I was made to understand I could live as long as I wanted to—and my guitar was smashed, a cop smashed it in with his foot, right while I stood there crying and trying to explain to them—"I'm a song-writer," I yelled. "I'm a musician!" The place was all wrecked by them, mattresses lying around and garbage all over, the dead ocelot I had to kill—had to smash its brains in with a lead lamp-stand, when it went crazy one night— the ocelot had started to rot—and I wasn't feeling well, staggering around and trying to wake up, and the bastard cops break the door down and arrest me— "Who are you threatening?" they asked me. "Is your name 'Bobbie Gotteson'? You're under arrest—you're being charged with extortion and felonious assault and trespassing and refusal to vacate the premises of a private establishment—"

I put up my usual fight. I'm a good fighter. I learned in prison to…to not give in…not to snitch, and not to give in… But they worked me over and when we got to the station I puked all over the stairs going in, and they gave me hell for that, and there was so much vomit and blood I couldn't talk over the telephone…trying like crazy to get through to somebody, to get a lawyer, to get a call through to somebody for help.…But my mind caved in. So when they said, *Hey boy, you greasy hairy little spic, hey, you going to threaten any more white ladies?*—I got it confused in my mind with being ten or eleven years old, a skinny little freaked-out runt back in New Jersey, with my drunk old lady yelling at me one day in the hall outside where we lived—and—uh—it all got collapsed into itself, the different times, and I was saying to her that I could fire her up and the whole building if I wanted to, if she would just stop screaming, stop screaming!—but that was when she ran for the police, my own mother, and came back with a cop from two blocks away, that was directing traffic out in the middle of a street, and madder than hell, a big, bull-sized Irish bastard, and my mother yelling for everybody in the building to hear, "Arrest him! Arrest him! He threatened my life!"

…So the cop said, "Boy, did you threaten this lady's life?"

So I said, "No."

She slapped me and said, "He tried to kill me—he's a born killer!"

The policeman slapped me when I tried to get away. "You tried to kill her? You tried to *kill* her?"

She was breathing so hard it turned into sobbing; then she staggered and pressed her hands against her stomach.

The cop knocked me back against the stairway railing. "Got a knife, kid?—huh? You got a weapon? Where is it? Where is your weapon?" He squeezed me. Squeezed my legs up and down. Yanked at my shirt—tore it across one shoulder. His face was red. "Trying to kill people, huh? Off to a good start in life, huh? Little wop!"

8
An Unfilmed Love Scene

The drill bounced against my tooth. An upper back tooth.
Everything narrowed to it, it was a little island of crazy
bright whining pain, but I sat very straight in the chair
with my hands gripping the armrests and my feet flat on
the platform, so I wouldn't go crazy and start kicking, but
the thing in my mouth…it was a hooked plastic thing that
caught onto my lower lip and teeth to drain the spit away
…the thing didn't work right and got crooked, and water
dribbled down my chin, and more water with a metallic
taste began to form in a puddle at the back of my mouth,
so I began to choke and the dentist said, "Hold still or I'll
drill right through your cheek—" and there it went again,
the whining pain like fire right up into my jaw, screaming
like a jet, right up past my jaw and into my head—

"Hold still! Hold still!" cried the dentist. I could smell
how he was sweating. He was a fat, angry man, out here at
the prison on Wednesdays, with a lot of work to do, and
his stomach pressing against my forearm, my forearm was
bare, my sleeve was worked up to my elbow somehow with
all the tension and pain, and when he paused with the drill
I opened my eyes to get some reality, some contact, but the

pain dizzied me so I could only see the wavering wiggling lines of pain, out there, in the air. A thing had been yanked down in front of me, with a light shining out of it, right into my eyes. The dentist was muttering to his assistant, a plump soft-looking plain little girl with a pony-tail, "Go get me some...hand me that thing...what's slowing you down?...I've got six more of these to do this afternoon, hurry up!...his breath is so foul I may lose my lunch.... You're going to have some real trouble, my friend," he said to me, angrily, making the drill buzz against a piece of metal, "just wait till that rot hits your nerve canals!...you never brush your teeth, *of course not*, which is why your teeth are green and your blood stream polluted with decay and your gums...Jesus Christ, your gums would make a display in a special issue of *Dental News!*—" Here he began drilling again. It was a different drill now, a low rumbling whirring one, very strange, coarse, like a sloweddown saw, and his voice got mixed up with the whirring— "All rot! Rot! *Rot!* They expect us to drill out the rot and get the hole clean and fill it in again with silver, do they, eh?—and all this standing on our feet for eight hours a day five goddam days a week and half a day on Saturday—and who is it for?—it's for criminals, rapists, murderers, and potential sadists, like you, what's-your-name, cringing in the chair—lucky for you this isn't an electric chair, eh?— or maybe it is?—eh?—they say the electric chair gets it over quick, too quick for some of the disgusting bastards who get strapped in it, in my opinion, and in the opinion of a lot of others, frankly, but *this* is one chair where you don't get it over with quickly, is it, my boy? Is it? Hold still! This doesn't hurt and you know it. You're a coward. The last man in here, he fell asleep under the drill—*fell asleep*—because he trusted me, he didn't flinch against me, he didn't set himself in opposition to me the way you are—Betty, hand me that towel. What the hell?—where is this blood coming from? Betty! All right now, sit still, it slipped a little but who's to blame, eh?—with you wiggling all around in the chair like a little weasel—lucky for you my schedule is packed or we'd have to do something about that wisdom tooth on its way down, it looks crooked to me, if the X-ray machine was working we'd get the low-down on that little number!—now this might hurt a little, because the hole is exposed now to the air and—"

I began screaming.

When the screaming stopped I could hear it echoing. The dentist was backing away. "I'm through!" he said. "Call the guard and get the little bastard out of here! I don't have to put up with torture in the line of professional duty—this is going too far—this is an outrage— And my stomach hasn't been right since he came into the room, his breath is an outrage—"

The side of my head by the tooth, the right side, on up and through the back of my skull it rang with pain, all pounding and fizzing with pain, and inside it someone was yelling at me: "—could puke, the creatures I have to treat! —could keel over and *puke*—and now he's got an exposed root and it serves him right, let him feel some human pain for a change, instead of stinking up the place with his

49

pyorrhea and his armpits—the little ape!—if the tax-payers of this state could peek in the door here and *see* just what their money is being poured into, the kind of rat-hole their money is being poured into—"

The girl helped me out into another room. I staggered, I couldn't see right. My eyes were filled with tears. Another prisoner on his way in gaped at me and said, "Jesus Christ..." and whimpered, and the girl let me sit down for a minute because my knees felt wobbly. She said something to me but I couldn't hear. I was hunched over, both hands pressed against my jaw. The girl was standing over me, wringing her hands the way one of my mothers did. She was saying, "Aw heck, hey, don't cry—hey—hey, your name is Bobbie, ain't it?—Bobbie?" She came around to face me, squatting down. She stared up into my face where my eyes were out of focus. Her thighs stretched the white material of her dress; the skin of her throat and her face was so soft, so soft-looking, one touch would mar it, one poke of a finger would destroy it, her lips were pink with lipstick and were murmuring words I should be hearing...."That wasn't fair of him, I saw what he did, he didn't freeze your gum and that was a dirty trick...just to save a few minutes, so he can get out of here faster....And that wasn't true, what he said about some guy falling asleep in the chair, well, that was a lie, it happened back in town with his own practice and the guy never fell *asleep* but had a heart attack or a stroke or something and had to be carried out feet first....I don't know why he tells such lies, right in front of me! I hate him! I should report him for drilling you without

Novocain, on purpose to torture you, then see how he likes it!" She shook her head angrily. Tears came loose in her eyes. A tear rolled down her cheek. She was my age, sixteen or seventeen.

But I hated women. On principle.

One of the exhibits is the Defendant's notebook of "obscene drawings." They are mainly circles meant to represent the female body. The circular parts are drawn lightly and sloppily, the other parts—the holes and slashes—are filled in brutally, angrily, blackly, and it is obvious that the Defendant broke the point of his pencil sometimes while drawing these things—When the notebook is shown to the jury, all the jurors gasp and look away, men and women both. It is shocking, and saddening, to see the graphic workings of a sick mind.

My Old Man up at that prison taught me how to hate them. Hate hate hate hate hate hate hate *hate* them Bobbie. Baby Bobbie. "Baby Bobbie Gotteson" was one of my names. My Old Man's name was Danny Minx also known as Danny Blecher and he warned me, he whispered in my ear in his meaty hot-breath warning, just a friendly warning, "If you even think about them, Baby Bobbie, I'll cut off your balls. How's that?"

9
Unfilmed Love Scene
In the Back Seat of Melva's Rolls-Royce

"You hate me, don't you? You hate women, don't you? Oh
you think you can trick me, squirming and writhing and
groaning like that, you're all alike, *you all share a filthy
little secret!* Bobbie! Stop or I'll roll down the window and
scream for help! Bobbie, this is not the place—this isn't
the place—"

"Yes. Yes. Yes. It's the place," I said, from the back of
my mouth, where the darkest sourest spit was gathering,
and I scrambled all over her and thrust my knuckles in her
mouth to quiet her because it was what came next; my
head was just open and receiving that day, and all that
remained of Bobbie Gotteson was the black poison at the
back of my mouth that I had to swallow so I wouldn't spit
it into her face, Bobbie in a dark red monkey-outfit with
gold buttons and braid, selected from a Novelty & Costume
Shop on Sunset Boulevard, by Melva herself, just the right
uniform for a five-foot-seven-and-a-half-inch chauffeur
with black curly wiry hair and black curly wiry chest hair
(showing at the top of his coat, where the first three buttons are unbuttoned) who has been waiting for two and a

half hours for his mistress to appear. Melva then did appear, making her way through the shoppers and tourists on the street, her hair now bone-white and not puffed out any longer but arranged in stacks like a wedding cake, little curls all around her forehead and hiding her ears, and in spite of the two and a half hours she'd spent in the beauty parlor I knew it was necessary for me to scramble over the seat and cover her with love-pecks, pouting puffed-up motions of my mouth, so that passers-by had something to see, even if this wasn't being filmed. Melva screamed. The car windows were up, the air-conditioning on, no one could hear her or if they could hear it wouldn't matter, I had the impression out of the corner of my eye that someone was even taking a snapshot of us—though I might have been mistaken—though Melva had the idea those days that one of her sons was following us around, jealously, and had put a staple into the front left wheel of the car so that the air dribbled out of it slowly and left it flat, for us to discover when we emerged from our bungalow at San Luis Obispo one morning. *Bobbie, my precious Bobbie, my brutal little Bobbie-glutton, wait till you get in show business—how proud I'll be, how the public will devour you!—just wait!* Melva teased me with the promise of a screen-test and a recording session, she whispered that she had a contact in Vanbrugh's studios, she knew all the executives there, then she whispered one night that she knew Vanbrugh himself, and in fact was an "ex-associate" of Vanbrugh's, she called him Vannie, and snuggled against me murmuring *Vannie, Vannie, all of you are alike, sweet*

*Bobbie-Vannie, you could be a son of his, you could be one
of my own darling boys…maybe I'll adopt you, tuck you
under my wing and into my will!—maybe maybe maybe
maybe—*

I wanted to rip the eyelids off her. First the left. Then
the right. Frosted-silver eyelids.

A pool gathered at the back of my mouth. Poison leaking
out of my gums, maybe. Greenish-black martini-sour liquid.
On the pillowcases in the morning there were black streaks
—but it was Melva's mascara, not my spittle.

"Oh you tried to kill me. You tried to strangle me,"
Melva sighed.

"Why not?"

"Oh you're getting like all of them, they go downhill
one step at a time…nastier, filthier…more demanding.…I
hardly know my own sons any longer," Melva yawned. She
shook her head and smiled vaguely at me. The drug was
taking effect. Her marred face, her sagging throat. "But I
don't mind. I'm tolerant of different personality types. You
wouldn't believe it…but back in the '30's I was a member
of…of…of the *Communist Party* out here, and I learned
to tolerate everything. But don't ever tell Mr. Vanbrugh on
me," she whispered. "If he found out he'd disown me."

I pretended to sleep. It was easier.

"I don't want to be disowned by anyone," Melva yawned.
The violence of her yawn ran through both of us. She lay
curled against me, her arms around my head so that my
face was loosely pressed against her throat, and we were
somewhere near the surf, the pounding of the great ocean

55

I had crossed this continent to see, or maybe we were huddled together in the back of the Rolls, parked there on the Boulevard amid the rocking thudding thumping rattling noise of cars and buses and strangers who gawked in at us. They too had crossed the great continent. To see. To stare. To take pictures of people like me. Half a block away was a famous restaurant humped like a hat, a brown hat, and if I raised myself on one stiff elbow I might be able to see if one of her boys was hanging out there, by the doorman who was supposed to be—how did I know this?— one of Melva's ex-lovers. The boys took turns spying on us.

10
How the Maniac Gotteson Travelled West

I wasn't a maniac then. But it took me 21 months to get here.

When they let me out I took a job with a construction company in South Amboy, to wait for my Old Man to get free. He was up for parole in a few months. He said to keep out of trouble, Bobbie, or else—!—and sent word to a contact of his on the Outside to watch me, and to report back to him if I got in trouble; so between the contact who was invisible and my parole officer I knew it was wisest to keep out of trouble. *But I couldn't tell them apart!* My Old Man Danny Minx floated everywhere, invisible, and in jail he'd taught me the powers of the mind and how he sent himself out of his body at will, to roam the streets of the city and be back in time for wake-up at seven, to slip into his body and fool everyone. I don't know. Danny took me under his wing and protected me, so if he was lying or crazy or putting me on I didn't ask questions not even silently, for fear he could read minds. The link between us was very strong, but it ran from him to me and not the other way. I could get messages from him, but couldn't send any. One day hauling lumber at work I got a crisp startling message from Danny to *pursue my musical career.*

So I took guitar and singing lessons from a Spaniard who ran a music shop in downtown Amboy. $1 a lesson and I tried to get in for two lessons a week, to surprise Danny when he got out.

I hummed songs out of the air. I could "receive" words if I hit upon the right tunes. I asked the Spaniard, a little nervous guy, if that was how genius worked—he said it sure was—it *sure was.* One Saturday afternoon, he had me play the guitar for people browsing around the store, like a wandering minstrel, I strummed the chords I knew and wasn't too scared and sang whatever came into my head—

> *o you're eatable*
> *non-repeatable!*

—and one silvery-haired man in his thirties or forties asked me for my autograph and to have coffee with him, but he looked so anxious I knew it was more than just coffee he wanted, so I said no. My Old Man would kill me. He had already fucked me in front of two other guys to punish me. At such times he said he was from the "F.B.I." and would "take no sass!"

Danny Minx got out and broke parole to escape to the West, and the two of us drove out together. It took us a long time. I picked up a very fine, new, tight-handling Pontiac, that was parked on a residential street with the keys in the ignition, and in fact still swaying a little in the ignition, since the lady had just jumped out of the car to run into the house. She was sure on her way back again, so little Bobbie acted fast, and in an hour we were many miles to the west of that scene, laughing and treating ourselves to handfuls of chocolates. Danny Minx also known as Danny Blecher said that chocolate was the greatest potion and he had to eat a certain quantity of it every day for medical reasons, to keep his blood sugar level up. It was directly connected with male potency, he said, and I have always found this to be true.

Somewhere just the other side of Wichita the trouble began with Danny, who was forty years old or more, when he stopped to give two college kids a ride. They were boys with short hair and smiles and a sign that said *Going West?* They got in the back seat and the four of us chatted for a while, then Danny giggled and said, "You two wouldn't care to aid and abet a thief, would you?—in pursuit of his daily worship?" The kids laughed a little but didn't catch on. I looked over at Danny where he was grinning. He didn't glance at me. He offered a drink from a bottle of Muscatel and they took the bottle, but I could tell they didn't drink from it, one of them made a swiping motion with his hand as if to wipe the top of the neck clean, and the other giggled, but Danny kept saying certain things to them that they didn't catch onto, until finally I began to shout.

"I'll kill you! You know I can kill you! I can kill you!" I shouted.

Danny began to laugh.

"I can kill everybody! I don't need you! I don't need anybody!"

I shouted and began to pound the seat between us. I was wearing just jeans and a T-shirt and my forearms were thick with curly black hairs that scared the kids in the back seat, I could tell, and Danny glanced down at my hands with that sly sideways look of his, but I wasn't going to be silenced, and for the first time certain things broke free in my mind—shapes and thicknesses—like snarling dogs, bounding and jumping around—and Danny's head jerked back as if he'd been bitten by one of them. He began to talk me down. He began to sing a little song only known to the two of us, in fact it was my own song that I told him was dedicated to him, *you're eatable...non-repeatable....*

That song was stolen from me by a two-bit composer at Vanbrugh Studios. It is the background music to one of their movies. They stole everything from me and kicked me out and set their guard-dogs on me, but if Danny Minx could come forth to testify...to be a character witness...it would be made clear to the public how I was defrauded ...my talents exploited...."Eatable" is the background music to *Walking Ragged* but there are no credits attached to it, nowhere in the credits does it say "Bobbie Gotteson"....

Did I journey so far West, all the way across this country, only to be fucked on film?

The boys got frightened and said, let us out, and Danny speeded up just for a laugh, and the boys—*college boys!*—began almost to cry and wheedle and I leaned over the seat to shout in their faces. I don't remember what I shouted. I tore at them, lunged back and tried to get hold of their hair so as to bounce their heads together. Finally Danny was laughing so hard he had to stop, and the kids got out of the car and ran away, and left behind some books and a cardboard suitcase, and we sped off again with me yelling out the side window.

Later on I woke up and Danny was parked in a gas station. The attendant was a kid my age. Danny and the kid were talking about something, I heard a funny whine—like a hillbilly accent—and realized we were out West. I got out of the car. My legs felt strange. My whole body was stiff, my shoulders and chest felt tight, like armor, and my leg-muscles felt all bunched up. I couldn't remember what was going on. I think that was the newness of my powers, the fear of them I had then because I was just a kid, the way my mind could seize hold of reality and give a shape to it, to mold other people to my will; I wasn't used to it yet. I felt very tentative. Danny and the boy stopped talking and looked at me. In those days my hair wasn't as long and thick and curly as it was later, when I got into private films and private catering to parties, when the styles in male fashions had changed, but anyway my black curly hair was eye-catching and I knew it and except for a bluish rough haze around the lower part of my face and going up almost to my eyes, from not shaving often enough, I was very handsome. It made me self-conscious. I walked past Danny without giving him a sign…and around behind the garage where there was a Men's Room…and when I came out I felt so good, so happy, I crossed a field adjacent to the garage and strolled up to someone's back yard....This was in Colorado, in the eastern part of the state. I don't know how I know this. The sky was bright blue, the clouds were just at the horizon, there were three or four little one-storey houses along a dirt road, clap-board houses, like shanties, and in the back of one of them a little girl was playing...playing with, uh, I think it was a doll...a naked doll...holding onto the legs and fooling around with it in the dirt....It was a little girl, I don't know how old. Two years old? Three? Suddenly I thought of how my powers, if unleashed, could rush out into that child and destroy her. She didn't see me. She had red hair, she was a little thing sitting in the dirt, fooling around. The day was very still. No, a dog was barking somewhere. Out on the highway a truck rumbled past. So powerful! So powerful! I felt the need to discharge my energies, I felt the building-up of powers that would make my skull go out of shape. I stared at the girl. Now she noticed me—she had felt my thought-waves! She left off hitting the doll against the ground and stared at me, and in that instant I felt my powers rise and flow over, like light if light could turn into water, fountains of water, rising and flowing over with love, because the little girl and I were looking at each other in that way, at that time. It happened *at that time*. Another moment, another heartbeat, and it would have been something else and maybe my powers would have killed her. But not *at that time*.

Danny came to get me. He said, "Hey Bobbie, why are you crying?"

I didn't know I was crying, I said.

"Bobbie, honey," he said. "Why hell! Are you crying because I teased you back there? Because of those plain, pimply-faced boys?"

I'm not crying, I said. I seemed to wake up. The back yard was empty, the sky was changed. Two dogs were barking.

Danny stared at me.

We drove on and stopped late in the afternoon for food, and pulled off the highway and down a farmer's lane that led by a railroad track, the car bumping along, weeds scraping against the fenders. Danny made cheese-spread sandwiches for both of us. We sat out in the grass. I knew something was wrong but didn't let on. Danny offered me some chocolates but I had no appetite. Then we both stopped eating and there was a noise somewhere like a train whistle or a coyote, and it made me shiver, because Danny was looking away from me and not directly at me, smiling dreamily at me, the way he always did this time of day. He cleared his throat. I remember exactly the words he said; he said, "Pretend you're in a movie, pretend you're a cowboy singing on the prairie." So I got my guitar out of the back seat of the car. I strummed a few chords and walked along, and began to sing, humming a tune until the words came out of the air to me…or maybe they came out of Danny's mind and into mine….

I heard him start the car. But I didn't turn around.

I had enough time to run back to the car, but I didn't. I didn't turn around. It was not the gun Danny carried that stopped me, either. That would not have stopped me. I don't know. I just kept walking along by the railroad track, which was raised maybe three or four feet from the ground, strumming the guitar, singing under my breath....I heard him start the car and back out. But I didn't turn around.

I got to the next town, then to a town after that. Then I got a ride all the way to Reno, where my luck gave out and I was arrested for vagrancy, because they were "cracking down" on drifters in that city. From there I got shipped to a mental hospital, where I made friends with a lady therapist who liked me, and it wasn't until I was released from the Nevada State Hospital and got all the way to Los Angeles that I found out that the President had been assassinated while I was locked up—by a maniac named Oswald, a two-bit punk who I was glad had been gunned down. That punk! That cheap Commie coward! I got hold of a picture of Oswald being gunned down, his face screwed up into a yell, him doubled over with his hands pressed against his stomach, and a sheriff's man starting forward to interfere with Jack Ruby—but finally I had to get rid of the picture because it made me so angry. *It made me want to kill someone.* I worked in Venice Beach for a while, just enough to finance my musical career, composing ballads in my head— "The Ballad of Jack Ruby" was one of them, but it wasn't one of my best songs—and wondered if Danny Minx would ever show up. I would have forgiven him.

He never came.

Or if he did, he had changed. His face had gotten fatter, his chest had gotten wobbly as a woman's. His legs thicker.

His voice shrill and cute, saying "Bobbie-this, Bobbie-that," and never letting me alone. Sometimes they followed me around, old guys, applauding when I finished a song and asking for a lock of my hair, asking for my autograph, pretending I was a star—and then kids followed me around also, mostly teenaged girls with long straight hair and big, moronic eyes, all in love with me. I saved money by sleeping on the beach at night. Sometimes in alleys or in doorways. I could sleep sitting up on a park bench and sometimes even with my eyes half-opened, in case a cop noticed me. Then one night in a bar in Venice there was a fight and somebody grabbed me, and the two of us fell and rolled over and over trying to smash each other's head against the floor, a stranger, a maniac I had never seen before, and when things got straightened out I was being booked for attempted homicide and my life caved in on me, and the Legal Aid man said to plead guilty because I had a record and what's the use?—so I pleaded guilty and the judge put me down for 15 years, without looking at me except a quick darting look that made his face squinch up as if he were about to sneeze. I wanted to explain that I was a musician and a troubadour and that my life was meant to entertain, just to entertain people like him, that I had a strong original talent that must be set free…it *must* be set free….

"Next case! Get that man out of here!"

"Your Honor—"

"Next!"

"Your Honor, please allow me to sing for you—"

"Get that creature out of here!"

11
Are You in Love
With Someone Who's Not in Love with You...?

About love they were never wrong, the old song-writers, the old commercial millionaire sons of bitches, most of them dead or dying off now in the Seventies and their mansions taken over by kids in their twenties....But they knew. They knew how it was. You love someone and he will not love you. He will love someone else. But that someone else will *not* love him. That someone else might even love you—! Or someone who looks like you. Gotteson was an original so hot-dark in the face, smouldering sullen gleaming glittering dark brown eyes, sideburns of black tough curly hair that inched down, down, down his muscular cheeks as the years went by and the Outside styles approximated the Inside spirit...just a few inches too short, so that even his three-inch cork-heeled fancy Italian shoes didn't help, during the brief time he wore them, clonking around town. *Why was he born so short!* But his legs were muscular, hard, they didn't seem to be made of flesh like other men's—*Bobbie, you are so strong!*—and his shoulder muscles were bulging on that trim, tight torso, though he did only fifteen-twenty minutes of vigorous American push-ups every day. His secret was not in his body. In fact, he scorned the body. He *scorned* it. Gotteson made love to the spirit, he sang his melancholy-cheerful ballads to the spirit, and that was why inmates (during Amateur Nights) rolled their eyes and made sucking motions with their mouths, while he performed, those long-drawn-out years at Terminal Island. And when he was Outside, when he walked out with several ten-dollar bills and two changes of clothes, he saw with amazement that the world had caught up with him...all the dreams had caught up with him... maybe gone a little ahead of him, due to faulty development of conceptualizing abilities and disjointed motor coordination....

Twenty minutes after he had been released from prison, on the bus to Los Angeles, *on that very bus*, a small-boned lanky-haired knobby-kneed girl of about fourteen eased into the seat beside him, sighing, shaking her hair out of her eyes, glancing sideways at Bobbie with that half-startled half-cunning look they all gave him, and murmured something he could not quite hear. Gotteson, unused to the world, to the rattling of the bus and the rapid motion outside the windows, unused to so many people who were free, freely moving about the streets walking wherever they wished, and especially unused to the feverish smell of this young glittering creature, could not comprehend her words. He didn't dare ask her to repeat them. Bobbie and the girl stared at each other. Finally the girl said, smiling: "…running away, it's my first time. How about you? They tried to fuck my mind. Back there."

Bobbie cupped his hand to his ear. "Huh?"

"Back there. Back home in Del Mar. Tried to fuck my mind. You know. What about you?"

What about Bobbie?

He feared her and could not believe her yet she pressed into his sweaty innocent palm something she called *sweet-heart-greenies*, capsules she and Bobbie took together, to initiate a small friendship.

Yes, they loved him. He was never to blame. They cringed and writhed for him, they squealed, pressed themselves against him accidentally in crowds at Venice Park or in big jumbled weekend streams of tourists and lower class suburban sightseers along the Strip, couldn't get enough of him. Gotteson had to learn quickly to harden his heart against that horde, or his singing-potency would have been decimated years ago….He hated them. Hate hate hate hate hate hated them. No not all of them, but most of them—*sweetheart-greenies* wouldn't blur the image sufficiently because the terrible truth was that, inside the *hate*, like a tiny perfumy current making its way slyly up through an enormous gaseous poison, was something like *pity*. He knew them from the inside. He was crucified on the cross of his pity for females….

Had he not pitied Melva's whimpering, had he not stuffed his muscular arms repeatedly into that monkey-jacket just for laughs, I, Bobbie Gotteson, of sound mind though broken body, would not be trying myself for my life, beyond all the reaches legal and extra-legal of the Law: my life would not be this disjointed confession, but a series of haunting melodies joined to lyric language. But no. The love of human beings does us in. We falter, stumble, stoop over, steal fire for them and are punished, mocked, picked to death by tiny painted nails, ooooh'd and aaaah'd over by tiny button-like lips. From the tiny green capsules Gotteson was drawn, by one creature after another, into excursions of the brain beyond all his ability to recall. *Cranks, peps, cartwheels, coast-to-coasts, uppers, black beauties, turn-abouts, bennies, dexies, footballs, purple hearts, double-entries, toads, icebergs*...and more and more medicine; but such belongs to pathology and we are concerned with art.

Love did him in, does us all in. This includes Doreen B. who never saw him before, was a total stranger to him and he to her, before those tangled shrieking five-and-a-half minutes of his hacking her "to death" (as the papers express it, not knowing that all deaths are suicide, especially newspaper deaths). Sorry sorry sorry sorry. This includes as well Sharleen M. who will not testify against Bobbie in spite of the Prosecution's sly plans. *Never.* They gloat, whisper among themselves, prepare their useless strategies...the District Attorney visits her in hiding, strokes her baby-blank face and her long hair and woos her famous mama and papa and keeps telling them *All is well, the State of California will triumph!* Will it, eh? Will it? Mama and Papa M. are not exactly the parents of Baby Sharleen;

Mama is the mother, but Papa the step-father, third in a series. The original Papa is in France making a movie, or at least that's what Sharleen told everyone, though everyone told *me*, giggling, that this Papa was in a mental hospital right here in town. But Sharleen is not going to testify and it is useless for the Prosecution to gloat over her. She will not testify against her beloved Bobbie Gotteson.*

At Terminal Island, Bobbie could have been an Old Man to any number of guidance-craving kids, but his spirit always yearned upward, he desired only men twenty or more years his senior, gentlemanly men but not too gentlemanly, tough-voiced men who were yet elegant, like that Judge who put him away for so many years. Exactly like that Judge! He composed songs for them, secretly. For them. For abrasive-eyed cynical-mouthed gentlemen with class, like Vanbrugh himself, though Bobbie only crept into the presence of Vanbrugh once…or into the presence of someone said to be the great Vanbrugh. Even now, melancholy-cunning, he is composing this jokey confession mainly to win the heart of the Judge who will sit above him, glancing at him or not glancing at him, smooth-shaven, cold, deathly, deathly-smiling when it is necessary to smile, a gentleman, a graduate of a Law School whose

---

*Though Gotteson wrote these ominous words 18 days before the news of this tragic child's suicide was released, he seems to have been absolutely certain she would not testify. Readers are not invited to speculate on the true identity of this child, though the "Mama" referred to has obviously made no effort to disguise her involvement with Bobbie Gotteson.

very name would be so foreign to the Maniac that it would send him into a trance....Gotteson's personal tragedy, in contrast with his professional-social-artistic tragedy, was that the gentlemen with class who glanced at him and then *gazed at him* with immense interest were never the gentlemen he, Gotteson, gave a damn about. It was the others he yearned for. Women, all women, any-age-women stared at Gotteson and in a matter of seconds sank into a kind of open-eyed trance, sometimes offensive to him (even a maniac has some moral values), but sometimes exciting, for despite his aesthetic distaste for females his body often acted on its own...perhaps cynically?...perhaps with a sense of humor...? But in his deepest clearest soul Gotteson could never never once not even once cajole his intellect into taking any of these females seriously. The one who died beside him and whom he did not abandon, she alone whom he did not abandon in her death, breathing bleeding herself out into the bedclothes, was not truly female at that moment...not female, not trapped in being a female...in *that*. She had been, like Gotteson himself, a creature of pure...pure....

But of that revelation Gotteson cannot speak.

So his tragedy was that he loved people who did not love him. We call that *irony*. And, conversely, he was con-temptuous of people who loved him, especially those who crowded and lunged and pawed....In Gotteson's heyday on the Strip, when he strummed his battered old guitar and sang wildly-ecstatically into the sweet dark smoke of Lucky Pierre's, among his fans there were even intellectuals

hungering for him....Disguised in out-of-date hippie costumes, their prescription-lens aviator-sunglasses sliding
down their perspiring noses, saliva oozing into their
square-cut rakish beards, men of middle-age drove long
distances to wonder at Gotteson's talent, revealing themselves clumsily but charmingly, in as much privacy as
Gotteson allowed, as professors...their interest in him
only academic of course, of course...though one, quite at
a disadvantage in the clutter of Lucky Pierre's, wept and
pawed at Gotteson, *Why did I spend my years with Jane
Austen, my God why, now it's too late*, passed out on the
dancefloor, a pity. Good graying still-trim men from the
great institutions up and down the Coast, Santa Barbara,
Santa Cruz, Berkeley, Palo Alto, San Jose, Riverside,
Stockton and Westwood alike....But though they hun-
gered for Gotteson he did not care for them; he disdained
neurotics.

Why is love so elusive, so hard-to-come-by? Melva
often glared and pouted, a winsome grimace out of a 1946
movie of hers that (according to a woman-friend) had
almost *but* not quite won her an Academy Award...in a
novocaine-frigid lisp declaring: "Why anyone in her right
senses should fall in love with a motherfucker like you is
incomprehensible. Almost a joke. Sickening, actually. I
don't know what civilization is sliding into." Propped up in
bed, she sometimes read and reread old *New Yorkers*,
kept in messy piles beneath the enormous gaily-canopied
bed, as if she sought, there, in the decades-old cartoons
and the chaste harmless smudgeless columns of print and

advertisements for Tiffany knick-knacks, some coherent explanation for *what went wrong*. When most rattled, Melva sought coherence; and she wanted it gracefully worded. *What went wrong with an entire culture! — a beautiful gracious sane sensible non-syphilitic subscribed-to invested-in way of life!* But in the end as always she would giggle and toss the rumpled old magazines back beneath the bed and snap her fingers for her Bobbie, as always. *O you beast!*

At this point the courtroom lights are dimmed. The fifteen-foot-high windows are covered with canvases to shut out light. The Prosecution — the District Attorney himself and two youngish ambitious assistants — now cause to be shown to the cleared courtroom that notorious underground classic "17 Mannequins & a Guy," said film purchased by the District Attorney's office through a secret series of negotiations with the director who filmed it (at El Portal, though background shots that might identify El Portal have been carefully blurred or blacked out), a director of international fame whose works have won awards at film festivals everywhere — Nice, Rome, New York City — but whose name is strangely missing from the credits. In fact — there are no credits! Not even the star, Bobbie Gotteson himself, is given screen credit and was certainly cheated of payment for his exhaustive work in the film as its central character, its musical director (the guitar-playing in the background is entirely his), and its inventor (though no film script as such was ever committed to paper); but it is no coincidence *that the film's value sky-rocketed after the arrest of Gotteson, from a paltry $500-a-night rental fee to the undisclosed fee which the District Attorney obviously paid into the Liberated Arts Talent Agency that handled the film....No coincidence, and yet Gotteson never got royalties, must sit stricken with shame and rage in the courtroom and witness his own public degradation, see there on the portable screen his handsome swarthy face and body going through its performance for an audience of people who can only gasp, snicker, wheeze, mutter "Oh my God—" or "Stop it!" but in no case, not in a single isolated case, give credit where credit is due and ease the Maniac's frayed nerves with a round of applause! The film runs for only 18 minutes (one minute to each of the dressmaker's dummies and a half-minute at start and finish for artistic zooming shots) yet by the conclusion the Maniac is weeping with exhaustion and despair. The Defense Counsel, sitting stonily beside him, inches his chair a little away from the Maniac. Gotteson weeps in his isolation, inside his vacuum, where he has always wept and where no one filmed him. And if he had been filmed, if his private spiritual life had been committed to film, it would have been his usual luck to be handed merely a cash payment of $700 and a few free meals and someone's year-old car...!*

The District Attorney, flush-faced, strides before the jury and has no need to shout now, since everyone is hushed and palpitating and dare not look into anyone else's face; he has only to go through his rehearsed phony-understated routine and call their attention to the *inhuman monstrous-*

ness of that behavior, the *inhuman energy* of that behavior, the *inhuman depravity* recorded there…and especially to that sword wielded by the actor in the last half of the film, the very machete here in the courtroom, *the murder weapon itself!* "The accused seemed to go into a trance, seemed to swing into a…what shall we call it?…" (and here a phony eyebrow-twitching pause, during which the Maniac wants to scream but manages to sit rigid) "…a sword dance, a fertility-rite-mating-dance, so bizarre as to make us doubt our senses, and obscene beyond any human ability to fathom.…You saw, ladies and gentlemen of the jury, how viciously the accused hacked that last mannequin to death—I mean, to pieces? You *saw*? You could not fail to *see*?"

One of the lady jurors is weeping into a handkerchief. The gentleman beside her, sweaty-faced, offers to lend her assistance, but is rebuffed, and blushes violently. The heaviest juror, a fairly young man with sideburns nearly as long and twiney as the Maniac's used to be, before his arrest, is breathing so heavily, his fat chest rising and falling so laboriously, that it seems for a while he may have a seizure of some sort. He closes his eyes; droplets of perspiration run down his face.

The District Attorney strides to the Exhibit Table, seizes the machete itself, and swings it around him with a violence that makes people gasp, though the Maniac is contemptuous of *that* machete, that piece of metal, knowing that it bears only the crudest resemblance to his magical weapon. *He could never use it the way I did*, the Maniac whispers into his attorney's ear, and when his attorney edges away an inch or two, not looking at him, the Maniac says fiercely, *and neither could you!—or anyone else!*

12
Gotteson on Film

A legitimate film-test did take place. It took place at the Vanbrugh Studios. Gotteson was invited to play the guitar and to sing as many of his compositions as he chose, and everyone in the studio congratulated him afterward, *everyone*, though no witnesses can be assembled now to testify that this screen-test did take place and of course the film has been either destroyed or sold as a collector's item to some wealthy Hollywood Hills connoisseur of the arts, name and address undisclosed…without a penny of the profits going to Gotteson.

Ten or eleven or twelve films, no-rehearsal films, partying films, some of them made when I didn't even know someone had a camera, one of them a joked-up version of that commercial for potato chips that has all the camels and the Rajah with a sword, and one of them a hit-off from a 1939 Dracula movie Sonya C. showed at a party at her house, and oh God it all came back to me in Hermosa Beach where my own bride bled to death beside me and couldn't even say out loud how she loved me or forgave me, it flicked back to me like a playing-card, just the way Dracula what's-his-name sobbed because his true bride died, and left him, that was how I sobbed too but nobody filmed that.

But....

But there *was* a real screen-test. They swore it was real. They were very nice to me, asking after my health, they were very polite and thoughtful, and Vlad J. seemed to be impressed with my performance. He promised that he would *personally* screen it for Mr. Vanbrugh as soon as possible. That screen-test did take place. And now if only ...if only someone would come forth with it, if only it could be located, if only a group of directors and movie producers and people in the industry would acknowledge, publicly, maybe even sign a petition to be published in the newspapers, that the boy did have talent and might have become a Star, yes, a Superstar, if moneyed interests and circumstances had only favored him! Otherwise Gotteson's private hopes will go down in history as *hallucinations*.

13
Why I Hacked
Nine Women to Death

The "hacking" was only physical and incidental. Don't ask me about the "hacking"!—my body took over, and when bodies take over the spirit sails over the horizon. Pounding, plunging, plummeting, fucking, hacking, what had it to do with *Bobbie Gotteson*, who existed in the realm of spirit? I didn't kill them alone, either, but had disciples to help me, every blood-splattered exhausting moment. The stewardess who crawled under the sofa to observe me was *not* hallucinating when she said there were three or four or five of me, bounding everywhere around the room. She was correct. My disciples sprang out of my head when I willed them into birth, they sprang fully-formed though not all of them were my size or age (in age they ranged from nine or ten years old up to twenty-five or thereabouts), and not all of them were equipped with machetes. The smallest and puniest of my disciples, a boy who bore only a coarse resemblance to me as a child, had to tear into his victim with a dime-store jack knife. That accounts for the confusion about "weapons." It explains why the witnesses who saw me depart from the bungalow saw *one man* (swarthy, about thirty years of age, 150 pounds, dressed in white trousers and a red-and-white polka dot shirt—an outfit belonging to one of the girls) while the surviving stewardess saw *a number of men.*

But all that is bodily, messy, disgusting. I don't care for that part of it myself. The various messes of the human body, though natural enough, have always caused me to cringe and reach for my guitar, in order to transcend physical distress. Atop a rumpled stained bed I have been known to compose an original ballad, swiftly, flicking my hair out of my eyes and strumming wildly in order to transcend the field of battle. *Bobbie, you are so beautiful!* some of them cried.

So it wasn't bodily. No. It was spiritual. The great moment was the one in which I felt my opponent's ego collapse...I *felt* it, though each time was quite different from the others. In some it was the gentle sighing-out of a soul through the mouth...in others it was the popping of a tough, stubborn structure, like a plastic bubble...and though I did not inflict destructive harm to the actress Irma R. that night at El Portal, I felt the *click!* of her ego as it broke...it was no surprise to me when I learned, a few weeks later, that she had died in a sixteen-car smash-up on the Santa Monica Freeway, initiated by Irma herself when her car swayed a few inches to the left as she drove at eighty miles an hour. It wasn't just women, either, though their egos were of course joyous things to smash, but men here and there throughout my life, who died in my arms or before my eyes without shedding blood, without the loss of a heartbeat, but who died nevertheless as Gotteson's ego soared. They gathered themselves together, adjusted their clothing, wiped their foreheads—and walked away! Yet their souls had been smashed, smashed utterly. The way that cop smashed my guitar.

Eye-to-eye Vanbrugh and I regarded each other, and *he* was the only man I couldn't match. My gaze swerved and muddied, confronted with his. I failed. I loved him. Melva's sixteen-year-old boy, Curly, had a pill-fevered glassy slack-jawed control that almost threw me—like staring into the eyes of a corpse—but I managed to burn him down, the little bastard. And at the Stauntons' campaign party for Senator Rutland up in Wildrose Canyon I confronted a rival who tried to woo Melva from my side, a platinum-haired boy with twitchy jaw muscles but steelish eyes I somehow thought I had confronted before, maybe Inside, or maybe at one of the psychiatric units I did time in, and for several tense moments it looked as if the little bastard might win....But he didn't. He lost. He faltered and dipped and broke and was ground down to nothing by Gotteson's will.

When I die, it will be by a shutting-off of my energy valves *from within.* I will decompose while they stare at me, trying to pump life back into me so that I can be returned to Death Row, and what a commotion it will be, rushing me into the emergency ward to get my heart started again before my brain pops too many cells, what noise, what fury, what a clanging of bells and screaming of sirens! But since my energies arise entirely from my soul they are controlled from within; and no technological wonders from the Outside are going to juice me up again. Let the District Attorney (wired to react with rage) protest all he wishes, and even threaten to bring malpractice charges against the physicians who labored to save me but of course failed!— for though Gotteson slipped up a little in being born, he will not err in his dying. All death is of course suicide. So we have Gotteson in his triumph....

The Assumption of the Spider Monkey.

14
Soul-Programming

Danny Minx sometimes known as Danny Blecher sometimes known as *The Eye* taught me to program my soul;
but joked so much, tickled me so much, that the lessons
never exactly sank in. Not until I was alone in California,
hitch-hiking up and down the coast, sleeping on the shell-
hardened sand, edging up to drive-in restaurants to see
what I could find in trash-cans or to beg little short-skirted
waitresses for hand-outs, and not really until I made my
way along the Strip seeking a job, did the conscious utiliza-
tion of Soul-Programming techniques come to fruition.

Those big beautiful billboards on Sunset Boulevard helped
me. I don't know exactly how. Helped me tune into something, latch onto something, the way my guitar strummed
on its own…receiving words for me as if words came from
outer space to me alone, because I was worthy of receiving
them. I could set my soul-program for *Introspective-Shy*
or—*Volatile*. The entire world was open to be imagined
in those days. *Genius, Gentle.* Or *Genius, Mad.* But the
summer of my ascendancy, the four-nights-a-week gig at
Lucky Pierre's, I set myself to a style indefinable though
some might call it *Sloe-Eyed Gypsy, American.*

85

When Melva and her friends met me, though, they pinched and nuzzled and tongue-tickled me for *The Outlaw, The Devil, Sheik*, and other corny old-lady ideas maybe taken from the movies or TV, and it was just to shock them and maybe disgust them (Melva and her lady friends like being disgusted) that I told them I was in essence a Spider Monkey, in my soul, with a looping furry cunning tail scrunched up inside my trousers. Melva shrieked with laughter and said, Jesus, her boys had been right about me, they'd picked a winner this time—those devils! She was very fond of me. She was fond of me from the first. I completed her trio of boys, shorter by some inches than the kids themselves, and the three of us could go anywhere, publicly observed and unsuspicious, Melva herding us into dairy restaurants and into coffee shops and into Venice Park funhouses, tanned and glaring-beautiful in her leggy billowing pants, all of us set for *Family Fun.*

But I was her chauffeur at the movie premiere where we chatted with Richard S., the talent scout who handled Fritzie D.B., that mascara-dripping mush-mouthed little singer whose fifty-foot face I had to stare at, across from Lucky Pierre's all summer long: how I envied Fritzie D. B.! Like me he was over thirty but like me he looked about nineteen. But droopy-eyed, mushy-mouthed! The bastard! And with Richard S. in one corner of the gay-lit theater lobby I deftly switched to *Substitute for Fritzie*...? And it was uncanny, how Richard S. got that message. He really got it. He stared at me, blinking, while Melva chattered away, and even took out his eyeglasses and put them on, to stare at me all the more, while I gazed eye-to-eye with him sending message after message, *all of which he received.* I know it. But Fritzie D. B. is still living, still alive, still recording his songs and collecting gold records, a millionaire at the age of thirty-one; it was his agent who died, found dead of an overdose of something, at his boat-house in Malibu. By then it was too late for me anyway, I'd dropped out of that world, by then...I think, yes, by then I had already slipped into my destiny....

I had programmed for *Revenger*. And *Hero-of-Headlines*. And even *Sex Maniac*. And: *Spider Monkey Triumphs*.

15
Above the Sea

—fifteen hundred feet. The air was wet. The sun came out a few times while we were there but in other parts of the sky everything was wet and heavy. Fog moved in like a wall but somewhere else, where I didn't think there was a horizon, the sun was setting. The reflections of the sun jumped back and forth and made me dizzy.

I said to them, I hate this place. I hate the wind up here. So I stayed for a while in the front seat of the Rolls-Royce, where I had sometimes slept anyway, just to be alone and away from their noise and their grinning. Melva came out to me, walking barefoot on the sharp-edged gravel, wincing and whimpering to get my attention. "Bobbie, there's a rainbow. The sky is filled with a rainbow. Bobbie, don't you care?" she said. I lay with my head down on the seat, not sleeping or trying to sleep, only blank, blanked-out. While she tapped at the window it began to rain again. She had a whining singsong voice not meant for me to hear: "…engagement or adoption?…Engagement or adoption?"

Some of them said, Go on and get engaged to him!—marry him!

Others said, Adopt him!

One of her sons wanted me as a brother. He thought it would be fun. The other son, the zonked-out one, the one I sometimes feared, wanted me as a *father*. He tugged at Melva's bracelets and whispered so that I could hear, "I want a father. I already got one brother and I hate him. Now I want a father. I don't remember my father. I want a new father—I want Bobbie as a father. I want him. I want *him*." Glassy-eyed, droop-mouthed, he grinned at me and seemed to be seeing things in the air between himself and me.

The little bastard. He'll be the first to go, I thought.

16
Hitting Off

Some of them were shooting at the hawks. Paddy and
Colette and June and a girl named Irma, who went a little
crazy, imitating the birds in their wide-winged evil circling,
in a dance she made up as she danced on the flagstone
"landing terrace." Melva was very jealous of her. Vlad J.
following us all over with his hand-held camera, one of
Melva's boys climbing down through the rubble to the
beach, slipping and cutting his bare leg on a rock, blood
swarming out. I laughed and climbed down to rescue him
—this was the second day and I was still powerful—and
tested out his blood myself, dipping a forefinger in it just
for wild laughter, and the kid went white.

At night you could hear rattlesnakes. You could hear
slithering and cold evil crawling. The inside of the place
was so jumbled, so smelling of wet people and their things,
that I went back out to sleep in the car. I like to sleep alone.
Out there my head was filled with the pounding of water,
pounding pounding pulsing of great waves, water breaking
against the beach against the boulders. The boulders were
big as houses. I cast my mind back over the partying and
the filming and wondered: Was Gotteson like that foam
down there, churning out of the Pacific Ocean only to be
sucked back into nothing…?

Vlad J. said he couldn't see except through his camera. Couldn't see things in three-dimensional focus. His eyes fastened on mine, through the camera lens. He said, Bobbie you have the most fascinating face, Bobbie, your face is… your face is fascinating.…Your body is fascinating.…You climbed up here, didn't you, climbed up from the beach or out of a hole in the ground, with little bits of dirt clinging to you, clinging to the hairs on your body, your fingers itching to get at us…?

I did the Machete Dance for him. Irma ran out to join me, eyes closed and stomach bared. *Do it, do it!* she begged. The others took up the chant. But though I was high from hitting off the blood a sweat broke over me and I went cold. Irma screamed: *Do it to me, Bobbie!* Floating in the pool and cast in a heap at the end of the pool were the mannequins from yesterday. Irma was like foam being churned up and flung at me, her mouth twisted, saliva running from one corner of her mouth down her chin, the others were gathered around chanting and stamping their feet, sweet Bobbie and sweet Irma, why not…?

Why not?

Somebody said that the scavenger birds could see death, could see life about to *click!* into death. That was why they circled El Portal all the time. Their shrewd lidless eyes were like mine. Could pierce surfaces that are a riddle to ordinary vision. There, there—there the fizzing-out of life, and *there* Bobbie swoops down to his target! Irma rushed at me. There were black smears around her eyes, her eyeballs were watering, itching, reddened. She was going to die anyway in a few weeks. The sea and sky and these chanting hoarse people were too much for her…she was someone's ex-daughter or ex-wife…she was "under contract" at V. Studios and hadn't had a job for six years, assigned to wait, she had wept into my ear the night before of how she had been a Queen somewhere—Davenport?—Davenport High School?—a *Queen*—and her beautiful face and beautiful black mane of hair had won her so many prizes and loves and this contract under Mr. V. but now she was a very old woman, ready to die, she was twenty-two years old and please, Bobbie, would I kill her so that she could break back into tiny particles of moisture…? She threw her arms around my neck but I swung the Machete clear of her with a trick I had, so that people gasped, and if I had not been so steady in my center of gravity she would have knocked us both into the pool.

At this moment the sun broke clear. Vlad J. ran up to us. "Oh, the sun! The sun!"

We rubbed our eyes and put on dark glasses.

Everyone denies these accusations, Bobbie. You are telling lies.

He came down himself. He came to visit. *He* came to visit. El Portal is in his name, you can check it—

El Portal is not in his name.

He came himself to visit, there are pictures of him! They all got out their cameras. Vlad J. filmed the landing of the helicopters. I was there. Someone ran to wake me up, I was lying in the main living room, with my head in the fireplace where the stone was very cold and restful, and I ran outside in spite of how burning the sun was, and there the first helicopter was landing....I went wild with it, the roaring and whining! I was very excited! Everyone had been arguing—would he show up, or wouldn't he?—even though it was Melva's birthday and some anniversary of theirs—but one of Melva's boys had confided in me that *he* had forgotten all about Melva, that *he* was in love with someone else and would never show up at this dump.... But he was supposed to come to meet me. This was to be our meeting.

You really are a maniac, Bobbie. It's pathetic, actually. That you, a no-talent two-bit three-time-loser punk from New Jersey, a State-supported little ungrateful bastard with fake gypsy eyes and a voice like coffee grounds—that you of all people should fantasize a meeting with the millionaire-industrialist, millionaire-inventor, millionaire-philanthropist Vanbrugh!

The first helicopter landed on the terrace. Some men climbed out and circled the terrace. I was a little off my head from the roaring because I hate machines. *I'm* no mechanical modern man! They were dressed in suits and ties and knew their way around, Melva invited them inside for a drink, but they said no, they didn't have time, but had to clean things up a little for Mr. V. who would be landing in an hour, and everyone looked at everyone else—scruffy and red-eyed and wild-haired from the night before—and Irma started to cry and staggered back to the house. I smoothed my hair down with my hands. They got the Mexican servants to clean up and one of Mr. V.'s aides and myself dragged junk out of the swimming pool, he was very polite to me, and appreciated it when I said I'd wade in, to get some bottles and parts of dummies' arms and legs that were floating around, so he wouldn't have to get his shirt-cuff wet. Then they sprayed. They explained that Mr. V. was very cautious about scorpions. I followed them around and helped move chairs and tables and beach-umbrellas. I said that I had a magic way with poisonous things, that I could pick up a scorpion and talk it out of stinging. It was a matter of inner rhythms. It was a matter of slowing your brain-rhythms to such an extent that the scorpion swayed with you, hypnotized. They were very polite to me and—

Bobbie, all this is a lie. You know that you never met any of these people. They deny it. Most of them deny it. And if you weren't under indictment for first-degree murder, for having hacked to death one Cynthia Pryce of Pasadena, California, you can be certain that the Vanbrugh Corporation would sue you for all you possess—

I did meet him. I met all of them. It's on film but I can't get hold of the film and I can't get royalties from it. The girl from Pasadena has nothing to do with it. I don't know her. I met her in a bar. She followed me out. She was a stewardess for Transcontinental Airlines and in my head I got it mixed up with *his* airlines—I hate machines and can't remember their names—something lurched up in me, like a log lurching up to the surface of some fast-moving wild stream, and I thought, Hey why not, hey, why not go home with this little doll and love her a little, and maybe, maybe she is a little girl of *his* to put in another good word for you, Bobbie?...because by then I was broke and desperate and everyone had slammed the door shut in Bobbie's face. Because I was sinking and bruised. I didn't know her name and in the bungalow, in the front room where she showed me all her girl friends' record albums, and we were fooling around, a mist came over my brain the way it floated over the railing from the sea. I got sick. Very sick. Throwing-up-sick. And so certain powers failed me and no soul-programming worked, and the girl started to throw herself around like she was crazy, and I was throwing myself around like there were many more of me, inside of me, crammed-up inside of me...like a woman stuffed with babies, baby rats or baby gophers or moles or...or things burrowing to get out, you know, and ready to use their teeth if they can't get out. When I came to the lights in the front room were smashed and the hi-fi was blaring, drums and rockets coming from two sides of the room, and I crawled over the broken records and the cushions with their stuffing hacked out and I saw this dressmaker's dummy with one shoe on and one shoe off and a lot of blood, and a weird red glow from the hi-fi where there was this little pink-scarlet knob, you know, made of plastic, that lit up to tell you that there was still electric current going there....My mind opened up a crack and alerted me to rise on one elbow, to look around for the camera. Was maybe somebody lurking in the kitchen, in the dark?...eh?...was it little owl-eyed Vlad J. who loved me so, and all but thrust Irma into my nest in the fireplace?

...or someone from the studio itself, The Studio, getting a few hundred yards more of film for them to scrutinize? But I didn't have my guitar any longer! I did have the Machete with me, which I usually carried wound in many yards of coarse woven cloth some girl gave me, brought back from Taos, to go with my primitive good looks, but where was the Machete...?

The dressmaker's dummy with all the blood was lying on it. The handle was showing. Weird-red, glowing-red, pink-scarlet-sinister radiance. It glowed in the dark. I crawled over to her and said, "Honey you didn't tell me your name, even," and it wasn't until later that day when I had escaped and was having a tamale-burger at a Strip drive-in, standing near some teenage bastard and his bright yellow Ferrari with the radio blaring, that I heard the news bulletin, but by then...by then the memory of it had all evaporated and I felt only that fuzzy little interest, you know, that you feel when you hear about four or five stewardesses murdered in some bungalow they rented out in Pasadena that the neighbors swore had been raided three times in the last three months for drugs and wild parties and late-night noises so I had only a foggy good citizen's interest in that, because my real self was with my music but my music was shut off and all those powers that went with it that I lost in the scramble-climb up Vanbrugh's house while those bastards stood around clapping and cheering and snickering—

Bobbie, you're lying. You were never at Vanbrugh's house: that house outside Lucia is not owned by him. Not

*according to the county's records. You didn't meet Vanbrugh,
not Vanbrugh in person. You met an aide of his. It was a joke.
It was a costume-party. It was a Mardi Gras party. It was a
joke set up by Dewey L. of The Studio to punish Melva for
her loudmouth talk about him having to sell his house and
move into a four-bedroom Colonial in the Junior Estates
sub-division off Mulholland Drive, because he was being
blackmailed through some convoluted contacts culminating
in a dead drug-pusher's close friend up at Berkeley who
possesses certain embarrassing photos involving the dead
boy and Mr. L.'s daughter....So it was all a trick, Bobbie,
to fool everyone at El Portal, just some actors dressed up as
Mr. V's flying squad and that degenerate decrepit character-
actor of the Forties, Edwin E. playing Vanbrugh himself.
What a joke! What a complicated maze!*

I looked him in the eyes. Eye-to-eye with him. I *saw*
him. I *saw.* They had to help him down the ladder, he must
have been unwell. He walked tilted a little to one side...
his right shoulder was higher than his left shoulder....He
wore a gauze mask that hid all of his face except the eyes.
One of the aides helped him...and he walked over to a
table they'd set up for him, the Mexicans all dressed now
in white, the blood- and gut-smeared outfits of yesterday
gone and clean starched white outfits on, white-gloved,
and even the slow-cruising buzzards seemed to stare down
at him. I felt my center of gravity tilt....I felt a strange tug-
ging in my brain, where so much had been hoarded up, so
much sanity and the need to run to someone and seize his
ankle and howl like a wolf, to surrender oh sweet Jesus at

last…after so many years…to surrender instead of having them all surrender to me, turning themselves inside-out to me and their shallow little dark crevices wet-aching for me, *for me*, the way a few weeks later all their moist little pores would be crying out for me to open them, but when *he* came to me, when the second helicopter landed and the hurricane-whirling subsided and his nicest politest young aide in a blue suit and a dark blue necktie and a white shirt led him over to the table, even though he was an older man as I could see, and walked unsteadily, and his gray-black hair was thinning so that an oval of his scalp showed through, *so very ordinary* that the terrace and the helicopters and the broken-up towers of fog coming to us from the ocean were changed into something else, the cries of the birds changed, everything shrill and breathless and burning with sun, and where oh God was my guitar?—where had I left it?—when this happened I knew I would never be the same again. I stood there hypnotized. He sat down, he looked at us. One of the servants uncorked a bottle of water and another servant uncorked a bottle of California wine and, while he watched carefully and indicated with a deft movement of his forefinger—he wore dark gloves—how high they should pour the mixture in a goblet, I seemed to hear the thought-message shooting around into all of us: *Stay where you are until you're released!*

17
Gotteson's Pilot-Film

They came into motion again.

It began to pulse with time and waves again, and little tentative giggles from the girls. And sound began again. And he motioned Melva over and for forty-five minutes she crouched beside him, not daring to sit, and the two of them talked together in whispers and I saw her face change and age and wither and turn greenish-metallic and brighten again and turn into the face of a twenty-five-year-old girl smiling glowing up into the gauzed-over face of a gentleman who had descended to her from the sky and would soon ascend again but in the meantime was almost touching her, almost touching her tear-sparkling cheeks, while the aides moved among us and said cheerfully, Don't just stand around looking so scared!—let's have some nice music piped out here or maybe some of you could entertain—*he* doesn't like anything fussy or fancy, just tap-dancing or even ballroom dancing if there's enough room—his tastes are very simple! We were all shy until Paddy cleared his throat and said, Hey Jesus, this sure takes me back, and he sucked in air for two-three-four laborious seconds and licked his lips and fastened his blood-cobwebbed gaze on a point just a few inches to the left of Mr. V.'s table and began a little dance-routine that I had never seen before in anyone. He lost his balance and started over. Someone said, You've still got it, Paddy! And someone else, a middle-aged tear-brimming blonde who had nibbled my toes the night before, snatched off her shoes and began to match Paddy in his dance, spreading out her arms and fixing a sweet glassy smile on the distance, and the two of them danced carefully, grinning, at first pretending not to be aware of each other and then coming together face-to-face with a foot or more between them, while Colette hummed very loudly and broke into a song that the others joined—

A one, a two, a dippety-dippety-do —

And where was my guitar?

Vlad J. slid his arm around my neck and said softly, "Honey, let's swing right into a proposition we've all been meaning to make you, and now is the perfect time, let's explore the possibilities of a comedy series in which you play the role…a timely role, and I have the go-ahead from a very interested producer at The Studio, unfortunately not with us right now, but a quick telephone call would get him out here fast if he *knew*…who happened to be here. Anyway it is a most timely role and Melva balked because she has this mania for troubadours, I mean the funky gutsy strong stuff, but I'm going to go over Melva's head and take the chance and put the proposition to you, man, because I know you don't have an agent, don't believe in agents, but look here, honey, the idea some of us cooked up together was: a comedy series with you as the star's side-kick, the one who gets all the laughs or most of them, the one who sort of steals the scenes, you know, up until the last five minutes when things straighten out and the drama gets prepared for The End, but anyway you've got this incredible natural fantastic talent for being so goddam funny…I mean aside from your other talents…but this is going to be a family show, you know, on television. On television. And some of us thought, Jesus, it was almost a spontaneous group-thought, that I should do maybe a pilot-film while we're all together out here, like a family, pretty well-acquainted by now and not so self-conscious, and now with Mr. Vanbrugh among us, what an ideal opportunity!—I make enough in six weeks to finance me the rest of the year, so I can do the kind of film-making I really want…and the kind that is somehow in my nature…*my unique inexplicable nature demanding to be given visual form*…And so, honey, my proposition to you is—"

I pushed him away.

I turned and ran back toward the house.

I was already crying, hoarse angry sobs, and behind me they stopped singing and dancing and said, "What…? What's wrong…? What happened…?"

I ran through the foyer and slid on the white fur rugs and almost fell, my eyes were blurred with tears, and righted my balance and ran through the big sunken living room and along the hallway past the Spanish tapestries and icons and in my rage I knocked a statue off its pedestal, and ran into one of the back bedrooms and tore at the bedspread, a heavy primitive quilt with cougars and American eagles and fir trees woven into it, and threw the pillows around tearing one of the pillows with my teeth so that fine white fluffy pinfeathers swirled everywhere, and I heard someone calling after me, *Oh Bobbie!* and my mind blanked out and I tried to crawl under the bed, because I remember lying under there with my eyes shut tight to keep the tears back and dust-balls drawn up to my mouth when I breathed in and pushed a few inches back when I breathed out, and Melva herself was kneeling by the bed and saying, "Oh Bobbie, did he hurt your feelings...? Oh Bobbie! Oh Jesus, I told him to let me talk to you. He's a Russian, he's never learned the nuances of our language...don't pay any attention to him, Bobbie, please come back out...please don't cry...Mr. Vanbrugh saw you run away and he's *very*, very upset, he can't stand for anyone to be sad in his presence, he's a wonderful and generous man and so seldom meets interesting people like us, he's usually surrounded with that squad of Harvard Law bastards that you can't get through to save your soul.... Bobbie, sweetheart, are you listening? Mr. Vanbrugh himself wants to see you perform. *Mr. Vanbrugh himself.* He's asking for you, he's out there actually requesting that you come back...he was angry with Vlad for upsetting you, and Vlad may just be out of a job if one of Mr. V.'s aides takes a dislike to him, but you could make us all so happy... and yourself so happy!...if you'd just come back out, honey, and show us how funny you are. There's no story-line cooked up yet, for the comedy series, and they don't have a male lead but it will be no trouble to find one—some tall blond clean-faced boring kid, maybe a surfer, or a singer with a good voice—and *you*, Bobbie, would be the scene-stealer! Did Vlad tell you all this? Honey, please come back! Please forgive Vlad, in front of Mr. V., so he won't get in trouble! We're all like a big family, even those of us who don't know one another well, it's all one party, honey, and please don't be uppity....Mr. V. had the idea that you were one of my sons, he seems to think you're a bit younger than you are....So come back, honey, let me wipe your face...that's my good sweet Bobbie, yes...yes, crawl back out here....You've been crying and your face is all dirty. Let me just wipe it clean, honey, so Mr. V. can see how striking a face you have....Such personality! Such bone-structure!"

18
Louise D.'s Birthday/Deathday

Telepathic nudges and winks drew me to her.

I can alter my own blood chemistry to release Truth Serum into my veins, in order not to lie, because I despise liars and would not stand among them. I don't lie. It was telepathic beams that drew me over there, and no old grudges against her. I didn't know her. I had only met her through a pal, who'd been her patient at some hospital or other, and he introduced us one morning at somebody's house-party, and kept saying, "Louise, you'd *love* Bobbie! You could *never* psych out our Bobbie!" She was taller than me, which I didn't like, and too loud and robust and joking, in her thirties, high on something or other and sounding off about some bastards in the legislature who were trying to cut back on mental health funds, which might mean she'd be out of her job, whatever it was, and she kept swaying and putting her hands on me, but I had my eye that morning on a skinny-legged small-faced blonde with mournful smudged eyes who was barefoot and lonely and needed taking in hand for a weekend, maybe, and so I didn't pay Louise D. much mind, because I had enough of big energetic cheerful-weepy women with Melva and her friends though somehow I liked Louise D. and had the idea, well maybe, maybe if she was my sister or something, she'd help me out, talking confidentially and quietly the way that lady therapist had talked to me out in Nevada: I had appreciated her interest in making me well. But it was crowded in the house and the skinny blonde was also eying me, sending little terrified dart-messages of *Help me, love me, take me in hand*, so Bobbie excused himself and headed for the little girl. And he didn't regret it either because she turned out to be Baby Sharleen and an important contact.

But Louise's liquid-bright eager eyes sank into my soul, so that I dreamt them out clear one night when I didn't even think I had been sleeping, when I'd already lost the guitar and was lying under some bushes in a park with my book-bag under my head stuffed with my personal possessions and the Machete, of course, inside its yards of special Indian cloth. This was three or four or maybe five days after the Pasadena bungalow and the girls who turned out not to be stewardesses for the right airline, but all that was foggy and insignificant.

I saw Louise D.'s eyes turning onto me. Focussing. I sat up and rubbed my face.

At first I did not recognize the eyes. I let them focus inside me. I didn't prod myself, didn't ask questions. A spark of excitement began, but I paid it no mind. I was done with loving. ("...farewell to love/loving...") The love-power would not last me, not since I toppled off that tower or turret or whatever people called it at El Portal, clamber-climbing up the vines that turned out to be bug-eaten, while the audience cheered clapped urged me on, consumer-bastards—and so I set my mind fiercely away from that part of my body. Though nobody believes me I must repeat for the record: I never valued such behavior.

Muffled outraged incredulous laughter in the courtroom.

I didn't! I didn't value it!…Everyone else did, the girls and the women and the spectators here in Court and the slobbering old-young men, even Danny, even my master Danny, but *I never did* because it was monkey-antics, monkey-tricks, black-spidery-monkey grappling and wrestling to earn a few bucks, however you lyricize it. Except for the immediate loss of my contacts—how they all deserted me, the pricks!—I didn't mind the fall and the shock to my vertebrae and my glands and the part of my brain that secretes the power-juices, I didn't even mind all of them laughing…though sometimes that raucous laughter returns to me here in my cell or in Court.…*I didn't mind* that crucifixion because Mr. V. alone did not laugh, though it could be argued that he engineered everything. No, for the record it must be said that I did not mind anything that happened to The Spider Monkey. But my music, my powers of music!—my soul!

Did you have the idea, Bobbie, that Louise D. would help you?

Yes. No. I don't know. I thought…I thought maybe… maybe a big girl like that, a big-sister, maybe she'd…she would sit and make me tea or something and I could explain to her about the guitar that was smashed, and how my contacts were all out of town when I called them, and how Melva had flown to Majorca with her boys and some-one else whose identity I couldn't learn, because people were lying to me right and left!...and I could explain about the stewardesses and how the amplified sound had given me powers I didn't exactly want, beamed in to me from some rock-group's soul, and how the Machete had acted of its own volition, hacking away and saying, "Who's your cute little monkey boy-friend now, honey, *who's* your por-table plug-in dark smouldering rent-a-monkey now?" while she kicked and tried to crawl out the front door....And it was a fiasco! A mess! And I thought that Louise whoever-she-was would understand all this, because she'd made such an impression on my pal that he talked her up often, and showed up at her apartment one night with a cop's helmet he'd gotten off a cop, him and some other boys, and kidded around with her saying, *Hey Louise! —we killed a cop tonight! —we killed a pig tonight, want to celebrate?—* And evidently she hadn't acted too alarmed, but asked the boys to please go away, she was so sleepy and the neighbors would be listening, they were nosey, please go away boys and no rough-house, you don't want to get into trouble. So I thought I would run to her.

And did she let you in?

Oh yes! She opened the door and recognized me, she was like a nurse, a mother, a teacher, a big-breasted lady older than me and wiser, standing there in a green flannel bathrobe with something white and flaky on her face....

She recognized me right away. She said *Oh! come in, you're Jerry's friend the singer, what's wrong with you? —why are you looking so blue? Are you still playing at Lucky Pierre's? Are you alone?*

She poured us both a drink though I don't drink and breathed rapidly and noisily at me, her pudgy shoulders hunched forward, not to miss a word, and I told her weeping about the days I had to hide because I was so sick-looking and the scavenging I did in garbage bins out back of the drive-in restaurants and the supermarkets, pawing through the spoiled meat to get to the fruit and vegetables because I didn't want to hit off raw flesh without others around to move in rhythm with me, and she seemed to understand, and her eyes filled with tears when I described crawling into a Salvation Army pick-up bin (though this had taken place a decade ago, in Newark) to get a few clothes, and almost falling helplessly inside, and the terror I felt then, and my mind leaped around the kitchen where we were sitting and I had the sudden idea that *this kitchen was familiar to me* and that the words I uttered here would be taped, recorded, somehow preserved in someone's memory who was not exactly here in the room with us, but maybe connected with this Louise D. who worked for some mental research clinic and could not be trusted....My mind skittered onto one of my mothers, and onto another of them, and focussed again on Louise D. who was staring at me with a small strange smile that showed just part of one of her big milky oversized front teeth, and I heard her saying, "Bobbie, don't be afraid now, Bobbie, Bobbie why don't you just…just sit still.…I have this friend, this doctor-friend, I would like to call, who can administer something to you to, you know, help you sleep if you'd like to sleep, on my sofa maybe, you're certainly welcome to sleep on my sofa…I'd love to have you rest up here.…So if you'd just relax and sip some of that drink, or maybe you'd like some milk…I could warm up some milk…some chocolate milk.…And then we could talk about this more quietly…and then… and.…"

But I interrupted all this. I tried to explain to her about the pilot-film, and how I had been doing so well standing on my hands and leaping about and when I began my climb, my monkey-climb, up the side of the house I had the audience with me all the way, breath-by-breath, and if she moved off that kitchen chair I'd slit her throat, and I didn't need any doctor-friend to put me to sleep, no thank you, though maybe I'd take her up on that offer of a nap on her sofa because I was *very tired.* She was about to jump up from the chair to help me, and I grinned at her one of my old slash-grins that must have been a genetic compulsion, a programmed characteristic, since I had never known anyone Inside or Out who could smile the way I did; so she sat back down again. She wasn't very pretty. I don't know why I had thought she was pretty. Her skin was yellowish the way Melva's was at times, early in the morning when her make-up was soured and filmed-over with perspiration, the way my tongue tasted at this moment, scummy and not well. *All I wanted, Louise, was to be a face on a billboard! —was that too much to ask?*

POEM FOR LOUISE

The Olympic swimmer swimming to triumph
The sparrow-hawk diving to triumph
Gotteson weeping in dustballs beneath a bed
or kissing hairs loose on a rug
or warm and curly with life
or sticky-drying on the Machete blade—

you did not look like the bastard
who gave me a hypodermic in Reno
or like "Louise D." on the front page
beneath the headline FIFTH MURDER
but like Gotteson craving crawling on the Strip
and like the Olympic high-jumper jumping
like Christ on the pole of All Knowing
we live right up to the last second
in one big triumph

I spoke to her evenly and quickly. I knew there was not much time. I told her that Gotteson without his guitar was deadly, that to brush against me would be like brushing against a scorpion, so charged-up, so coiled-back, and that my trouble had always been people crowding too close, causing static to interfere with my natural powers, falling under my spell and begging me for love, even for intimate little husbandly chores like plucking some woman's eyebrows for her in a steamy bathroom with music piped in ....I told her about the clinic someone had dragged me to, back in Newark, where I had to sit on a bench for an hour and a half, and where I wet my pants, and the other kids began to giggle, one of them a six-foot moron wagging his finger at me. The air in that stuffy steam-heated place had burst into pieces of knife-blades, flying everywhere, and not even little Bobbie himself could escape their wrath! *Louise, sit still, Louise, don't move.* She began to cry. She said that yesterday had been her birthday. I asked her, how old? and she shook her head slowly as if pretending she had not heard, and I said, honey, you don't look more than thirty to me, and she didn't take me up on the compliment but just kept staring at my hands, which I had to hold still to keep from moving hypnotically, a corny habit of mine I must have got from one of my show-business friends. I said, I bet she was very kind to her patients, she had that kind of cheerful big-sister look that meant so much to sick people, especially men. But the sparks-out-of-my-brain were a little too much for both of us, I think she could feel them, she began to tremble and just sat there staring at my hands, and I tried to keep my voice down because of the neighbors (somehow I knew about the neighbors being nosey) to explain that I was still that child on the bench in Newark, still innocent though fouling my pants and still being laughed at, though now that I was an adult I could strike back at those who laughed. She whispered that yesterday had been her birthday...and I said to her, now yesterday is over...it's three-thirty in the morning and a new day for you...and you didn't want another birthday rolling around anyway, did you?

In that kitchen both of us learned that God is a Maniac

like me: out-guessing and out-hyping me. My wildest soaring song came to me in a rush-of-words like a spasm *Hate hate hate hate hate hate hate pity.* You start with *Hate* and end with *Pity.* So I hacked her free of being Female, caught there inside a big bulk of raw flesh, scented with Lilac Talcum Powder from the corner drugstore, the two of us grappling and sliding around on the slippery linoleum, Gotteson knowing deep in his brain the truth of the words of a small cartoon-vision of Gotteson, instructing him that he *talked too goddam much and now look!* Yet I was out-guessed by the God of the Night, Gotteson himself outdone by the energies that came to him, and crept away exhausted and self-disgusted before four AM, with no one the wiser. If the neighbors heard anything they didn't let on.

Defense Counsel requests that it be stricken from the record that the Accused made any reference to "God." The Accused, that is, the Maniac, protests that at that time in his life he did believe, he seemed to have sudden knowledge of, the truth of God's Mania for Man, His Mania for All of Man (and not just Part), and God's being able to easily outstrip Man in Fantastic Imagination and Deeds. He meant to honor God! He certainly meant to honor God, as one Maniac honors another! — But the courtroom is noisy, the Judge is actually banging his gavel, the television cameramen don't know which face to zoom up to, the Maniac sits stricken and impotent in his sweat-drenched thirty-dollar suit, so baggy on his emaciated body and so different from the cruisewear he used to own only a few months ago. He cannot even remember a woman named "Louise D." and though he is not on trial for her murder (one woman at a time!) he is very sorry to have forgotten her. He remembers a green bathrobe. He remembers a slightly protruding front tooth.

And so, Bobbie, in your activities as a killer you followed the same basic pattern of promiscuity begun so many years ago, as a boy in Juvenile Detention...? Through you, or boys just like you, diseases are spread across the continent. There is an epidemic of diseases, isn't there? What we are asking you, Bobbie, is just this: to the best of your knowledge is it possible that you are only a pawn? — a tool? — that you and diseased boys like you are actually being used by intelligent forces to infect the American continent with debilitating and brain-rotting diseases...?

No.

But it is a possibility, isn't it? We find it remarkable that someone as degenerate as yourself, as mentally deficient as our records show you to be and your dull-eyed appearance argues you actually are, can answer that question so confidently!

Throughout my life I did worry about that—about influences. About the way the moon acted upon the ocean, and how it might act upon me. After the stormy session in Louise's kitchen, when I must have blacked out for ten, oh maybe fifteen minutes, and just seemed to fall through the floor and keep on falling, and threshing around, arms and legs, hacking and plunging and gasping for breath, oh sweet Jesus I had to take stock of myself. I was frightened. I begged for some change by the Brown Derby, where the doorman seemed to recognize me and asked how Melva was, and I lied to him and said she was spending a few weeks at a beauty farm north of San Diego, and hoped he wouldn't notice my unconvincing tone of voice or the nail-scratches on my face, and excused myself as soon as I had collected a few dollars' worth of change, and went to a flophouse downtown to take a shower and shave and I turned the water on Cold to give myself a shock; to make myself think. I had to think: *Which direction was I headed in?* It had always upset me to witness the strange powers of the moon, the rising and sinking-back of the tide, and to apply that to my own life, to think that maybe someone or *something* was influencing me without my knowledge. I had always received my music, gratefully. I had "received" it without question. But these recent events, the Machete leaping into such life, sweeping and plunging and pulsating and throbbing in a way the guitar had not, this frightened me because my soul blacked out at such times and abandoned me to whatever was going on. So I stood there under the cold freezing shower and thought of penance. Doing penance. Getting my mind straight and reason-driven, Bobbie Gotteson in his own head again, not running wild. I had a terrible vision of one of the chickens out at El Portal, running with its neck cut and blood flying everywhere, and how the girls screamed, and jerked their legs back so the blood wouldn't get on them, and I seemed to feel myself inside that chicken, running and squawking helplessly, and I thought of how one of my buddies at Terminal Island had explained to me how a kindly teacher of his once taught him to conquer his stammering: *by making himself stammer on purpose.*

19
Doreen B.

A penitential act. A Negative Act. An Undoing-of-Magic Act.

Why, I didn't even know her! Therefore, no personal motives. No personal revenge. She reminded me somewhat of Irma, though shorter and plainer than Irma, just a secretary or typist-appearing girl, that I followed home from the beach and saw how lonely she was, her heels worn down, and her bleached hair wilted from the humidity that day. I followed her right up to her apartment on the third floor of a walk-up, but she closed the door on me and for some reason I didn't want to knock, I thought she might stare at me through the peep-hole, and, somehow, *recognize me*, so I waited until dark and climbed up the side of her building, hand-over-hand, concentrating on not falling, on one brick after another, very slowly, cautiously, though there was no moonlight to guide me or to illuminate the blade of the Machete, as I pretended there was in my poem. In fact, the Machete was wrapped in its carrying-cloth and stuck in my book-bag, which had a strap so that I could carry it over my shoulder—

The District Attorney throws down his wad of notes, pretending to be at his wits' end and now embarks on spontaneous impromptu cross-examination, and even the front-row spectators look frightened and guilty, he is so angry, and he shouts in a terrible voice that echoes high in the ceiling of this 19th-century building, where airplane-propeller-sized fans rotate to stir the humid air: "Gotteson, just where did you come from? Just who are you?" (Someone at the back of the courtroom yells: "Out of the locker, you know where he came from!" and we all turn to see who it is, but the police have already ushered the girl out—she must be one of the "Liberate All Prisoners" pickets who are hanging around outside, complete strangers to me, and from what I have gathered the same rich kids who made my life miserable when I was begging for small change, seriously and desperately, while they were having fun putting their hands out to tourists—oh, what I could do to them all, what I'd surely do if I were liberated!)

In my cell I have thought about this. I "think" all the time, even when I am asleep. Or maybe it should be put differently—thoughts come to me, thoughts "think" me. Sometimes I am wrenched with spasms of thought-waves, running through me the way, in the old days, convulsions used to go through those I loved with my finest most meticulous style, during which time there was no "Bobbie Gotteson" any more than there was any human being there, the object of my love-power. On the Outside, concerned so much with my career and caught up in a frenzied rapid-living crowd of middle-aged people, mainly, except for the young girls whose sunken eyes were so middle-aged, I did not have time to notice all this. I thought that *Bobbie Gotteson* was doing the thinking. Now, I know better. Now, I know that *thoughts* are thinking Bobbie Gotteson; Bobbie Gotteson *is* a thought-spasm. Sometimes he is more than a thought, and sometimes a spasm.

Gotteson, just where the hell did you come from?

I couldn't come from anything normal and good. No. Because if I came from anything normal and good I wouldn't be the Maniac I am. But since if everything in the world comes from the world and is normal and good, I must be somehow normal and good…somehow or other. Lying beside that girl, the one I don't like to think about, all these spasms passed through my brain, and I saw Bobbie Gotteson at each step of his life…like on a stairway with real steps…Bobbie at the age of nine, Bobbie at the age of twelve, and on and on and on to where it almost drove me mad, *Bobbie my own age, Bobbie as myself!* Can you imagine what that would be like—to see how Bobbie Gotteson is your own age, the shape of your own body, his face the same face as yours, all of it squeezed into you and pulsing with life? Oh sweet Jesus, I would almost rather be back on that bench with my pants wet and people sniffing and giggling at me, I'd almost rather be back in Boys' Detention in New Jersey where some black kids dragged me into a stairwell and spread-eagled me and buggered me on our way out of the dining hall. I'd almost rather be gaping up into Melva's ugly sobbing face and hearing those words she spat at me, when she had to admit to herself that her Spider Monkey had gone the way of her other lovers, *just another puny floppy impotent white man!* she had screamed. That sinking feeling, that feeling of black swirling sick horror, the floorboards fading, the earth opening up to you, the way I felt when I heard what turned out to be the second stewardess out there on the porch fitting her key to the lock, oh Jesus, now for some inspiration!...and having to crawl to the door because I was so weakened by all the blood around me, even though it wasn't mine, and having to snatch at her ankles and yank her into the room, before she ran away, that incredible inexplicable feeling, that no song I could ever compose would get rid of. *Because there are some things that go beyond music!*

So, no. I couldn't come from anything normal, but everything is normal so I came from it and am normal. Unless I didn't come from anything and am not really here, though I seem to be sitting in an ordinary cell (not a padded cell since I am sedated) and I seem to consume the three-meals-a-day plus ten o'clock snack, and after my death professors at the Medical Institute adjacent to the prison will certainly do an autopsy on me....I am going to leave my brain to the Neuropsychiatric Department of the Medical Institute, and my kidneys and liver and heart and eye corneas to the transplant-experts there...and my life-story to Antioch Paperbacks* and Vanbrugh Studios, free of royalties or fees, I don't give a damn any longer.

*Despite his often uncanny powers of prediction, Gotteson was mistaken here. Homonovus Paperbacks and not Antioch will handle the unexpurgated *Confession.* Fritzie Del Blanc will play the lead

But where did you come from, Bobbie, and who are you?

Hate hate hate hate hate hate hate hate pity.
Pity pity pity pity pity pity pity pity hate.

The girl with the fluffy red bangs—I know I'm skipping one of them, but that session was almost all blacked-out—made me hate her at once, the way she pursed her lips and crossed her slender ankles…the hate swelled into larger and larger balloons of hate, I could hardly hold myself back from her even before we were alone, and I knew how I had to rescue her out of that sluttish outfit of hers, I began to pity her so, the two of us wept together when we saw how hopeless it was. Then she somehow freaked out on me, maybe a long-delayed reaction to some bright peppy pills she had taken before I strolled by, and she giggled and laughed and began to rock in silent spasms of laughter, *as if she'd done all this before* and couldn't take it seriously. She pushed past me and ran into her closet-sized bathroom and tried to get the door shut, but I shouldered it open, and she leaned against the sink and pressed her damp forehead against the mirror of the medicine cabinet, laughing helplessly, hiccuping with laughter. I shook her by the arm, I grabbed hold of her shoulders to shake her sober. *Stop that! Stop that!* But it was like one other time a girl had freaked out on me and almost ripped my left ear off with her baby teeth, nothing can bring them down, nothing except

in the film, produced and directed by Vladimir Jastsky, for Mega World Studios. The film is scheduled for release December 26 at major movie houses across the continent.

time, and Bobbie hadn't time to wait for her. So I didn't wait.
What—what are you?—what are you doing? she giggled
when I began but still she could not be serious, not even
my pity could make her serious, not even dying made her
serious, it was all screaming helpless laughter the way a fat
woman shrieks when someone is tickling her though this
girl was skinny and—

Then I ran out of the building. Down the front stairs
though there was also a back stairway. Right out front.
Running, slipping, gasping for breath, not caring who
might see me, anything to get away from her screams of
laughter. *They can't even die serious!* I remember how
Danny Minx was always joking. I remember all the jokes
and clowning around at El Portal, even when I asked them
to quiet down so they could hear my serious ballads, but
no, no, they wanted so desperately to laugh, the mechanism got going and couldn't stop until they passed out. My
mother, my original mother, did not laugh at anything. I
know this. When she had me they sewed her up with
coarse cheap black thread and there is nothing funny
about that. I learned how to clown around and entertain,
yes, but I never laughed much at my own jokes, and I
could see how Mr. Vanbrugh was a serious man—he alone
of the audience didn't guffaw when I fell backward and
nearly broke my spinal cord—he was a gentleman—in a
sedation-heavy sleep each night I dream of him arriving at
my trial and stepping forward to be a character witness—
though they said he had never appeared in a courtroom in
his life, had never been served with a subpoena and never

would be— *What are you? What are you doing?*—are not questions Mr. Vanbrugh would ever ask.

> *as the tiny fish float in the harbor*
> *belly-up and harmless*
> *so parts of our brains float*
> *in parts of others' brains*
> *and no one is to blame*
> *for that single immense triumph*
> *in which we all float*
> *belly-up*
> *and harmless*

ESCAPE IN BROAD DAYLIGHT
PASSERSBY DO NOTHING
TO HALT FLEEING KILLER

THE CURE FOR STAMMERING

—and for any other obsession—

MANIAC STRIKES AGAIN
AND AGAIN

—and again, though never with that daring reckless front-door busy-avenue escape, all of my disciples running and panting alongside me, bumping into me, Gotteson-as-a-boy colliding with a very surprised and angry black woman, last year's Gotteson (in his three-inch elevated shoes and the embroidered snug-fitting shirt from Tangier someone gave him) out of breath after the first frantic minute or two, his hand pressed against his side, whimpering with terror. But I, Gotteson-who-is-now, kept my wits about me and ran through an alley, climbed over a fence, jumped down, and ran down another alley like a fleeing suspect in a movie or in one of the Sunset Boulevard advertisements for a movie up there in gigantic color—the fleeing suspect with his back to you and a gunsight fixed on his head, through a telescopic lens. No telescopic gunsight was aimed at me. *Passersby Do Nothing To Halt Fleeing Killer*, the newspapers said angrily.

WITNESSES DISAGREE
Killer's description Uncertain

I ended up in Hermosa Beach. I had some money: there was a woman's billfold in my back pocket. I went to a TacoBurger place and sat alone in a booth and began to focus on the print in front of my eyes, someone's discarded *Los Angeles Times*, and I tried to get the print to stop shimmering, but for a while had no luck. I ordered a double TacoBurger with chips on the side and a Coke, but had no appetite for any of it, and asked the little-girl waitress if they had any chocolate bars for sale, but she said no, she looked surprised and said no. She watched me from behind the counter, standing there with something held up against her chest—it must have been a big menu—and the two of us were alone in the restaurant for a long time, maybe twenty minutes, and once in a while I would glance over at her and there she stood!—eye-to-eye in contact, a smokey-faced sixteen-year-old, maybe a mulatto, and I never touch anything except white people, a taste I share with Danny

Minx. She had thick wine-colored lips. She stared at me *recognizing me* and the air between us was pulsating with short sharp cries I could not interpret, and when I looked at the newspaper the print danced around to taunt me— *illiterate* I overheard someone say of me once, but that is a lie. I am not illiterate. I can read fairly well, if I am not being observed or crowded or jeered at. In the TacoBurger I seemed to be reading about a maniac-on-the-loose, the words jumped around, shivered, shimmered, then leapt into focus and were about an unknown young man in his late teens, thought by some witnesses to be black, by others to be Mexican, or Spanish, or Italian, or something familiar to the area but not familiarly-named, so there was disagreement and police were "baffled." One man swore to police that the "young man" was not a man at all but a husky young girl, dressed as a man. *She ran like a girl*, he claimed.

Except for my dizzy eyes I could take this without involvement. But my eyesight was failing. The girl came over to me silently and I felt her standing there, a little behind me, behind the booth I was sitting in. She asked me something. I couldn't make myself turn around. "...wrong?" she whispered.

20
The Redemption
Of the Maniac Gotteson

She was a long time dying.

No daring climb up the side of a building, no Spider Monkey illuminated by moonlight and cameras...not even any disciples, who leapt out of my head but grew dizzy and faded and failed and sank away as if into the floorboards of this shanty. I wrapped the cocoon around us. There were only two of us.

Jump-shots, athletic tricks of the camera, montage-freezings, no, nothing, only a cocoon for the two of us, for even my machete was lost—dropped on the stairway of that other building—and I had to use only a pair of scissors snatched up by chance, when the two of us knew all was lost. Except for the film or films the Prosecution will acquire and show in the courtroom, everything else is lost to the public, and the other films are on the black market, delivered by messenger hand-to-hand, and Bobbie Gotteson circulates underground without royalties or credit or public acclaim until someone, some night, shrieks with disgust and burns the expensive film while everyone else protests, *that collector's item!* and then all will be truly lost. Because

I came to think, I came somehow to know, that the screen-test Vlad J. gave me at The Studio in Hollywood was not a real test at all, there was no film, only a trick to quiet Bobbie down. Bobbie needed quieting down, then. Bobbie needed a fake film-test so that everyone could get out of town.*

She put up no fight. It was a sigh, an unsurprised clutching, a broken-off scream. I came at her while her back was turned. No screaming, no giggling. She wore a white slip. I thought of brides'-white in the movies, the costumes of girls seized and held aloft by Frankenstein or large apes and sometimes raised in the jaws of scaly monsters, a melodic screaming but no serious struggle.

I bundled her off to bed. I was not angry. I did not hate her. She was a long time dying and I did not know what to do, I had dropped the scissors and didn't want to crawl around to find them again, I was very tired, the signals coming to me were faint, fading away. Nobody shouted in this room. It was a back room in a shanty. My heartbeat slowed down. Sweat began to dry on me, all over me, so that I could feel it like a crust—slowly drying. I had never noticed that before. I carried her to the bed and lay her down and decided to lie beside her, just for a while, to get calm again.

Was there space between you two, Bobbie?

I gave her the one pillow on the bed and lay with my own head flat, I lay there not thinking or wondering, just

*For the record, Vanbrugh Studios deny both a real and a fake screentest.

the sweat drying on me, and if there was any pain to it, to all that bleeding, I did not feel it through her, she lay on her back and made only a whimpering sound, an *oh...oh... oh....* My heartbeat slowed down. It slowed along with hers. My pulse subsided along with hers. Except for the blood there was nothing that had to do with a body. I lay flat beside her and turned my head to stare at her, quieted-down but afraid, and I asked her did she feel any pain...? But she didn't answer. "Do you feel any pain?" I asked. "What is it like?" I asked.

She was older than sixteen. It said later that she was twenty-four. She was small-boned, smaller than Bobbie. Dusky-skinned. Dark-haired. Her eyes were half-closed but I could see that they were dark, probably dark brown, like my own. "What's your name?" I whispered. She did not answer. I could hear her breathing—quick short gasps— but both of us were slowing down, slowing, the signals that kept us in touch were fading. I raised myself on one trembling elbow to watch her. Her eyelids, her nostrils...her parted lips...and between us the soaking dark inkblot of her blood or maybe it was my blood, all my anger seeping out of me, fading, soaking into the mattress, pulsing out slowly heartbeat after heartbeat, helpless, coming to an end one ordinary weekday night, nobody watching, nobody filming, everything coming to an end. Lost.

I tried to stay angry with her. But. But it faded. I couldn't remember why I was here. I hated someone, but who...? I didn't hate anyone. I hated them and then I pitied them, but now I couldn't remember what that was—*hate*—or what that other thing was—*pity*. I began to be afraid. I said, "Why are we here…? What happened? What…what happened to us?" She seemed to hear me, she looked toward me, I saw her eyes shifting behind those dark lids….She groaned. She tried to speak. I said eagerly, "What, what did you say…?" but I did not dare touch her, I didn't want to hurt her. "Honey, I don't know your name! I don't even know your name!" I said. I could feel a heartbeat throbbing between us but it was not very loud. Oh sweet Jesus, what is happening…? What is happening to us…? I asked her what did it feel like, what was she feeling…? I asked her what was happening. Her eyelids fluttered. I could see her nostrils widening. She said something, I didn't know if it was meant for me, I began to panic that she would die before she could explain, and I cried so loud that it must have frightened her. "Don't! Don't leave me! Wait! Wait—stop—wait—" But I could feel her going away. I could feel the heartbeat fading. If I had not been so afraid of her I would have grabbed her head to hold those eyelids open, I would have held them open with my thumbs, *held them open*, but I couldn't touch her, I stared at her and began to cry, I said, What, what is it like, what is it…? What are you seeing…? Who is there, is anyone there with you, wait, oh God please wait, don't leave me…don't leave me….

"Don't die yet, wait, don't die," I screamed, I begged, I got up from the bed and hung over it, wringing my hands like someone in a movie, even the smell of blood and the wet soaked bedding did not disgust me, I begged her to look at me, to tell me her name, to explain all this….

"Why did you let me come back here with you, why did you bring me here, if you're going to die? If you're going to bleed to death?" I shouted. But she jerked her head on the pillow, her hands moved by themselves, no fighting, no clawing at me, she whispered something I could not hear but I was terrified to get close to her. "Wait—stop— what are you seeing? What's there? Where are you going?" I said.

I leaned over her. She said, "I...I...I can..."

"What?"

"I can see into it...."

"What? What? What? What? Wait—"

But she did not answer. I stood hunched over her, staring at that face. It was moving away from me...I could see it changing. No good, I could only whisper to it, to her, I begged her not to leave me but in a whisper, and she was gone, she stepped over into what she had been looking at and went into it and disappeared and I, I was standing there in a panic, Gotteson standing alone sweaty and trapped in his body, sobbing long ugly melodramatic Melva-hoarse sobs because he is Gotteson the Spider Monkey and nobody else is Gotteson and Gotteson cannot get born into being anyone else, Gotteson is Gotteson is Gotteson forever. In this cell, in Court, in a gas chamber, in a morgue, out along the beach, rinsing his mouth with water from a rusty faucet or strumming his old guitar, Gotteson awake, Gotteson asleep, Gotteson in his essence or Gotteson surprised in an uncharacteristic mood, Gotteson Inside, Gotteson Outside, Gotteson clambering up the wall or toppling back down, jeered at or applauded, bouncing high with green capsules or dragged low by the forces of natural gravity, all's one Gotteson Gotteson Gotteson unrepeatable. There you are.

I began to scream. I screamed at her. "Why?"

I ran out into the street. Palm trees along the sidewalks, ragged and spidery, a city-smell to the evening air, and I ran out stumbling and shouting "Where is it?—the ambulance? Why is it so slow? Why didn't anyone call the police? Where are you all?" I ran out into the street. A car passing at about 10 mph almost ran over my foot and I pounded on the hood, and the driver gaped at me surprised while I screamed at him, "Get the ambulance! Where are you all hiding! It isn't too late, help me! Bastards! Bastards! Where are you all hiding—?"

LOVE, CARELESS LOVE

O nobly born....

Now all his bones were broken, smashed, ground down fine. He could feel them, the powderfine bones. All was dry: dust inside him lining his dried tubes and sacs and dust outside him blowing listlessly, whining, howling but at a distance, no threat to him. Yet he was still courteous or frightened enough to ask: *Have I been here before? Does anyone recognize me?* He lay in a hallway, a corridor, unattended now and terrified that he would be jolted off the stretcher and spill, like sand, onto the floor, but he could not stop his voice: *Is this the same hospital I was in before? —they brought me in the back way but it looked different from this—is this a different place?* Someone yelled down the length of the corridor, but not at him. A sudden furious yell, a shout, and then the sound of doors being opened violently—but he could not see—he lay still, waiting, and then located an elbow, an elbow-bone still curiously firm and reliable; it was a small cup of a bone. He pushed himself up. No one pushed him back down so he looked at the jumble of people sitting on chairs and on the floor, lying on the floor, sitting fainting hemorrhaging quietly, a few like himself on stretchers. *Is this a hospital? I don't want to be here. If this is a —*

Lie down, someone said in surprise, be still, be quiet!— and helped him down and rolled the apparatus away, the ceiling now passing in slow uneven motion overhead, Jules trying to say *Because I don't want any help this time all I want is, please, please, I dont have any insurance anyway, all I want is the rest of it ground up fine, my head is too hard-skulled and filled with debris—I want it ground down to powder, to nothing—*

Toppled into bed, from a great sickening distance and into a bed, and clutching at the bed as if he were clutching at the smooth surface of a wall he cried…*Is that so funny? Don't laugh at me!* But they claimed not to be laughing, was it funny he should be looking for God down inside the much-laundered savagely-bleached sheets or in the cor-puscles of his own being, his dust-dry brain cells, no, they wouldn't laugh but held him still when he tried to raise himself on his elbow again, threshing his legs beneath the sheets, his feet a great distance from him and wasted away *I want everything ground down fine, burnt in the hospital incinerator and scattered anywhere* but someone said impa-tiently, bluntly—*you should shut up you bastard.*

Though he had often been addressed this way he was always shocked, each time was the first time, he sank back off his elbow, sank back, hurt, confused. The cavity at the rear of his skull, where dark scintillating thoughts swam, weedy and sticky, filled to bursting and he would have to lie there, in it *Help me please, help me out of this* and someone told him or a patient in a nearby bed that if you foul your bed once more you can lie in it, lie all night long in it, you pig—out here for the free blood and the free beds and the tax-payers' mercy, who is safe now, who is safe anywhere, be still or this needle will shatter your spine and the fluid will splash up to the ceiling—

But that was another hospital, another emergency ward, Jules' nose had been smashed, as he recalled—*Forget it.*

I want to forget—

A conversation over him, back and forth over him, not about him at all and punctuated by a girl's quick breathless laughter *I want to get out of this—out of this—* There was a commotion somewhere in the rear, a cart with a squeaky wheel pushed by, and another patient moaning, moaning *I want to get out of—* Swaying carts, ball bearings needing grease, whimpering flame-gutted people always demanding too much, too much, no wonder the staff yells for them to be quiet, the newspaper editorials warn them gravely, seriously, *in a democracy it is still required that*, the building itself vibrates with the ferocity of an avalanche of arms and limbs and torsos and gaping yearning mouths—

This will hurt a little.

Someone said: Lie back. Lie still. Let me examine you, please. Jules shivered along his length, boneless and obedient. His head was resting on a thick pillow. A piercing light was clicked on, shining into his eyes, sharp as the blade of a knife, penetrating his eyeballs back to the optic nerve…he lay unresisting, thinking back there *Let me die* and the person who examined him clicked off the light as if hearing those words

…putting the instruments away, sticking it into his pocket as if it were a pen or a lightweight flashlight, unfriendly to Jules he muttered *That was it.*

What?

That was it, the examination was it.

Jules blinked at the man glimmering beside him, an intern younger than he was, clean-shaven, dressed in a soiled white outfit…the man's hair cut short and not the grease- and dirt-stiffened mess on Jules' head, growing like wires out of his scalp. Now he saw the man's eyes neat and merciless and competent as those of a bomber pilot or a policeman or an actor impersonating an intern and he tried to ask, to concentrate his strength into a question: *What do you mean?*

The man's voice had dropped to a soft guttural confidential close-up movie-screen murmur, intimate and knowing, but Jules couldn't quite make out the words:…the light, the light I just gave you, that was *it.*

Jules saw him prepared to leave, he clutched at the man's arm, oh Christ don't walk away and leave me, but his throat was too dry, it tasted still like sand, don't leave me, give me a shot of morphine or sodium pentothal…like the last time, to help me confess…give me something to help me sleep.…And the man leaned over him to hear, his face perfunctory, dutiful, while around them people moaned and a woman cried out in a shrill voice for someone to get a doctor in here fast, God damn it, where were they, she couldn't handle this alone and Jules tried to whisper in the man's ear: Can't you...?

Can't you help us?

His tongue groped helplessly in the space where his tooth had been knocked out, years ago, and evidently the false tooth too was missing...missing again...and he didn't have the money to restore it, or did he?...he had a lot of money but couldn't remember where it had blown to.... But the intern was losing patience. He unhooked Jules' fingers one by one from his arm, he said *You're not going to die*

Jules clutched at him. *Not—*

It was fast, it went fast for you, the man said, that light I shone into you...but you did receive it, you accepted it... *let go of my arm*...now it's necessary for you to wait, you're incapable of dying, just remember that, and cruelly murmuring to Jules' stricken face *No you're not going to die, I predict you won't, not tonight anyway*— And then he seemed to be rearing above Jules and chatting in a normal robust joking voice, like an actor reciting lines that came into his head from nowhere, from anywhere, from Jules' feverish mind itself

> ...lie there and whine all you like but you're incapable of dying and in a little while...we're running behind schedule this morning because of strays like you...the Chief of Medicine himself will make the rounds and see what the ambulance delivered last night...but don't expect him to be in a good

mood, he hates it here however he pretends to like it, he'd love to head some clean 400-bed clinic in a village zoned against welfare where you're not in danger of inhaling syphilis when you do a routine examination…no sudden movements, you bastard! He won't be gentle, like me. He'll open his case of pins and see where the muscles are still working, he'll do a quick bedside autopsy on you, hand-over-hand he'll grab out your intestines but don't flinch because at that age, after so many years of charity work, he wants only obedience and no resistance and you must say Yes to him Yes to him and when he hacks out your heart don't flinch, it's a good idea to smile, yes, the way you are smiling right now, smiling and cringing in terror, the brain-autopsy will be ticklish, you'll experience an intense desire to sneeze but I caution you: Don't sneeze at that moment. You can imagine why. He'll then stuff everything back in, wind up the intestines as best he can and stick them back in…I'll be back to check later on so don't try to rearrange yourself, you know nothing about your body, just be quiet and smile Yes at us and what you feel now is a needle groping for a healthy vein…a healthy vein, in this corpse!…a healthy vein for the fluids to drip into because you're dried out flat in two dimensions don't twitch!—don't scream! It hurts, yes, but you won't die. You're incapable of dying. Even when you're hacked apart and burnt in the incinerator in the basement you'll revive again, you'll be back and now this will hurt a little…a little…. But you won't die.

TEMPORARY HELP URGENTLY WANTED
NO QUESTIONS ASKED

S. Grady   253-4232

There, at the bottom of the column of type, there, that was it.

Jules read the advertisement through several times, slowly. He had come to think of himself as temporary by now…a temporary human being. So this advertisement might be for him. Months ago he had thought sanely to himself *I want my fair share of everything*, but now he never thought such thoughts, they must have belonged to another person. Something about the brevity of this ad, *no questions asked*, corresponded to a brevity of his soul.

He was sitting in a square in some wind-blown place in the city. He had several dollars left. He got to his feet suddenly and what remained of the coffee spilled and the paper cup rolled somewhere beneath the bench and his mind leapt to the sunlit scarlet-blossomed ocean air and an empty rocky windy place off the highway….*She would ask him to turn off there.* And there, with only monterey pine and cypress and bright pink ice plant flowers and invisible birds around them Jules would make love to her, *Temporary Help*

No Questions Asked...and heaving and pumping and sobbing his very soul into her he would somehow see this Jules rising from the bench, the coffee spilling, the ocean not far away and the great boulders silent about them as they gripped each other....

Before Jules telephoned "S. Grady" he had tried other jobs. He had tried very hard.

He had bought all the Los Angeles newspapers each day, as early as they appeared, and he had sat somewhere, at first in a booth in a restaurant near the University of Southern California, because his seedy-glamourish, skinny-sharkish appearance allowed him to be a brother to many he encountered, and he had marked the likely want ads with a blue ballpoint pen, and later he had sat at a counter in a diner, somewhere marking them with a pencil he'd found in a lavatory, and later still he had gone through the want ads sitting at that end of a certain square where men willing to do lifting and moving and grunting work for union workers, paid high union-enforced wages and therefore free to cast about to see, Would any of you gentlemen like to make a few bucks and no questions asked...? drifted together, looking embarrassed and seedier as the day progressed, not meeting one another's eyes, Jules ashamed to be there and taking jobs away from such rundown sicklooking hollow-in-the-chest hacking-coughing old rummies, whose hands trembled so violently that it was no surprise when the trucks swung along the curb and the face leaned out the lowered window and shouted, Noner you guys, you old sonsabitches, get the hell away from this truck, I'm lookin for somebody that for Christ sake won't keel over and puke in the merchandise—

But sometimes no trucks showed up, nobody. No face, no bellowing voice. As it got to be ten o'clock, eleven o'clock, twelve o'clock, the men huddled and drifted and re-formed again at the northeast corner of the square, where office workers and occasionally even tourists came to eat lunch or feed pigeons or drop quarters nervously and eye-evasively into the outstretched palms of the non-unionized workers, but not Jules, who would be excited by now about certain promising advertisements—

DO IT NOW!
HOW OFTEN HAVE YOU DREAMT OF FINANCIAL SECURITY ADVENTURE CHALLENGE LONG-RANGE CAREERS?????
New Organization in LA seeks brite young indiv'ls high in reliability & common sense
   Call Al Hammon 463-8817

TRAINEES DESPERATELY WANTED $$ OPEN $$
  Top Firm seeks highly-motivated young males
  sky is the limit if forward-seeking
   Call Honeymoon Haven 886-8811, after 8 PM

  WE NEED SOMEONE TO LEAD CAMP-FIRE
  SING-SONGS FOR CHILDREN & OFFER
  FREE HOLIDAY POSSIBLE LOCATIONS
  ABROAD
    Call MK at 226-3831

ALL YOUNG GENTLEMEN & LADIES
WHO ARE IN NEED OF AN OCCUPATION
SATISFYING A THIRST FOR ADVENTURE &
DEPTH - FASCINATING CLIENTELE, AREA
& SAN DIEGO

Call "Huff" Wilson 324-1763 anytime

—and it wouldn't be until four or five in the afternoon when he gave up, exhausted, disgusted, tossing the thumb-smudged newspaper into a trash bin, and thinking dark smudged thoughts as he walked back to the Star Hotel, where he had a room.

He knew it was a phase in his life, a temporary phase. But the problem was that each day he got more smudged, seedier and less glamourish, sharkish about the face as his cheeks thinned and a peculiar bluish tone appeared on or in the flesh of the cheeks, darkening around his jaw and throat, so that it was sometimes unnerving to see a famished dark-eyed black-haired shadowy thing approaching him in a mirror…actually beckoning to him, half-smiling at him, rising out of the mirrors in public places that always seem to be speckled as if someone had coughed frankly onto them, and green-tarnished, because of the lead backing eating through the mirrored surface, and Jules had to go to that mirror and look at himself, blinking the occasional tears out of his eyes. The problem was that each day the phase deepened, darkened, each night at the Star Hotel was noisier, more desperate the sound of weeping in the room next door gave way to screams and to thuds and thumps and laughter, and when Jules returned one day, a more than usually promising day and therefore a more than usually disappointing day, the foyer was crowded with policemen and the desk-clerk, a part-time student at one of the local universities, ran over to Jules—they had become friendly though not friends—and warned him away, there'd been a murder up in one of the rooms, one man bashed to death and eight or nine other men, all living in that same room, under arrest. So it was that the phase of being unemployed worried Jules, because it was affecting his morale.

Through no fault of his own he had lost his most recent job—he'd been a factory maintenance worker—a janitor—because Handyman Enterprises had gone bankrupt over a weekend; he could not reason that such bad luck was his own responsibility, his fate. Before that he had worked for four days on an assembly line in a small parts factory in East Los Angeles, but his mind began to drift out of his body, his sweat-stinging eyes got blurry, he had been shoved accidentally into a hot soup vending machine by several workers in a fist-fight, and had walked out, not bothering to quit, had just walked quietly out past the armed guards and their cruel stares—his trousers wet and small pulpy *a's* and *b's* and other letters of the alphabet sticking to him. Before that, though not in this order because he had forgotten the chronological order, he had driven a truck for Ringle Refrigerated Foods and a taxi in the area of Venice Beach, where he was dragged out of his cab and beaten with a tire iron and robbed one Saturday night, and he had taken part in a sleep deprivation experiment at

UCLA which had caused a temporary amnesic reaction and other impairments that gradually faded, though he could sometimes hallucinate hypnagogic dreams even now —but always the same two or three, always Jules swimming calmly and sanely across a pool of water, or Jules seizing boulders in his bare hands and throwing them down into a ravine, Jules-this, Jules-that, frankly he was sick of his own dreams and it pleased him that, lately, he didn't dream at all. His initial job out here—he had come to Los Angeles from Detroit, some years ago—evaporated when funds were withdrawn from a federal poverty program, due to a general cutting-back of federal moneys, as they expressed it, in such areas as his own, and in mental health programs as well, but most immediately because Westwood and Los Angeles police had raided an apartment rented by one of the program's directors and had arrested everyone there, including Jules, for possession of narcotics....The charges were dropped after a while, but the program was finished.

With shaky forefinger he dialed 253-4232

> and someone answered on the first ring
> and asked where he was, and when he said
> the location the voice said, surprised,
> Hey that's right nearby, you must be
> the man.

Ganzfeld stared at him. Stared, blinked. Ganzfeld said, You're just the man....

What strange luck!

Ganzfeld explained, later, after his wife had that pre-monition dream about a long-haired lovely girl seized by that lovely long hair and flung up into the clouds that parted into the sun itself, he explained the last time they talked together that the other men who'd applied for the job had *all been spies*. All of them. One by one, spies, from other investigation agencies, intent upon learning Ganzfeld's methods and simultaneously sabotaging his cases and jeopardizing his professional reputation with clients and with local attorneys and with the police, one by one they had telephoned "S. Grady" and arranged for appointments, and one by one they had shaken his hand, one by one all that day, until Jules showed up, obviously not in anyone else's hire.

You're even from out-of-state, aren't you?—Ganzfeld asked kindly.

Jules explained that he had been out here for a long time now, and knew the city well.

Ganzfeld said he didn't have to know anything, he had only a simple assignment and it would be over in a few weeks—this was a very temporary job—and he, Ganzfeld, was only acting as agent for another agent, who sometimes sent work his way, because he knew Ganzfeld was reliable, but, excitedly, leaning close to Jules in order to whisper into his ear, Ganzfeld said he suspected he knew who the client was in this particular case...*he suspected he knew.*

Who?

Ganzfeld chuckled. Read about it in the papers, he said coyly.

WHO MUST BE MURDERED? said the picket signs
FREE ALL PRISONERS
ALL PRISONERS POLITICAL PRISONERS
LIBERATE THE PRISONS!

They picketed outside the courthouse where a trial was going on and one day Dewalene herself showed up down there, staring, weak from hunger and the noise of the street. As she stood, staring, the cap she wore to hide her hair slipped slowly off…and Jules watched, helpless.

This is my body and this is your fate, she said to Jules, walking head-on into the binoculars' lenses. Staring, staring, swallowing dryly as lust rose in him, blowing from one dry-arching crevice of his brain to another, he must redream that coagulated dream of her: O but you didn't love me.

He fell in love across the width of a street, across a ravine in the central city. Ganzfeld gave him the key to the room, "S. Alkon's" room, and there he sat for hours on the edge of an army cot, staring out the window, back aching, shoulder aching, his face split by jaw-wrenching yawns. He had not thought this job would be so boring. He did nothing, hardly moved; yet he was dense with fatigue. There came to be a dread needle-like prickling in his brain, the sensation he felt when in danger of falling asleep in some place he must not sleep in—a bus station, a park. The long undifferentiated hours threw up into his vision a girl, a girl lying on the carpet of that apartment, a girl entwined with another person, a man…yes, a man…yes, Jules himself…the two of them threshing about. Maniacs.

Yes, maniacs: let them tear at each other with their teeth....
the field glasses Ganzfeld had assigned to him lightened
with the hope of this vision and then became heavy again
as Jules' imagination failed and the window across the way
remained blank, blind, the ordinary dime-store shade drawn
down to the window-sill....He swayed toward sleep and
then forced himself awake, forcing up behind his eyes the
crude primary-colored fevered vision of a girl and Jules
gasping, struggling,

making love on the floor of that unseen
room: at first nudging each other's face, then bumping, then
mashing, then pounding, in an activity that began with an
ordinary chaste kiss, working up to a heated wordless
screaming bout until they lay exhausted, crumpled together
in full view of anyone who might be watching and Jules
stood in air trembling and had to lower the binoculars and
lean forward weakly to press his damp forehead against the
window-pane, soothing rot-soft enticing hypnotic syllables
rising to him in accompaniment to this vision, *yus, Julius,
jewel-yus, lus, ylus, Lyus*: *yyss*, hypnagogic incantations
to follow him to his death, and beyond....

Nothing can be annihilated, not even powder-fine
memories have no memory.

✤

The photograph showed an angular-faced young woman, the lips curiously strong, the upper lip rather short, as if raised in order to show the front teeth—which were a little crooked, for which Jules loved her because his own teeth were not American teeth, not the kind that are photographed. A striking face, not pretty. The eyes focused upon the viewer, penetrating the lens of the camera, making a kind of accusation: *Why…?*

Why…?

Ganzfeld met him for the second time, on a street corner. He wore a powder-green sporty suit but something about it was wrong, ill-fitting. A brown-green-black tie dangled six inches or more out of his coat pocket, like the tail of a satiny snake; he must have torn off the tie and thrust it in there. Middle-aged, anxious, talking nervously about the transaction, I'm just an agent for another agent and you're my assistant, and showing Jules the photograph—*Is that her?*—all you need to know is "Dewalene" and don't bother with accumulating information other than the comings and goings of…514 Prince Street and across the way is 511 Prince Street, Room 2C under the name of "S. Alkon"….

Is it a jealous husband? Jules wanted to know. *A divorce case? She looks about nineteen years old—*

They all do, Ganzfeld interrupted. Don't speculate.

Is she a model or an actress or a girl connected with one of the studios?

Ganzfeld moved his head from side to side, eyes shut. I don't know her, Ganzfeld said contemptuously, I don't know *any of them*. Missing persons, runaway persons, persons-about-to-be-slapped-with-injunctions, divorcées, thieving employees, victims, murderers, they come and they go, we get photographic evidence, evidence on tape, we guard them and escort them, we keep them under surveillance for months and then drop them when we're told to drop them. They come and they go, I don't know this girl and you won't either, don't ask questions, don't become involved, *they come and they go*. The wisdom of the profession is: Don't exaggerate the humanity.

She has such beautiful eyes, Jules said slowly.

They all do, said Ganzfeld.

Mournful and contemplative, like all savages trapped in the vision of others, there was "Dewalene" drawing the curtains aside, her hair longer than it had been in the photograph, thick and falling cleanly from an uneven part raked across her scalp. Being so pale, so hollow-eyed, she did not look like a girl from this part of the world. Though she could not have seen Jules she gazed at him, contemplating him, sorrow long-lashed in her, that same short upper lip raised, wondering, bewildered, frightened, *you are being watched, you are being recorded, you bear the invisible burden of a universe of witnesses, your womb is filled with them, you cannot escape....*

She had been in there, hiding in there, for six days straight.

Nothing has ever happened to me for the first time, Dewalene said days later, her cheeks tightened with the passion of a contest, an argument that might save her. Eager, tender, alerted by something in Jules that was— that might be—a way out of the truth of what she said, she was coltish and younger than her true age (twenty-three) and taunted him with memories of a great, three-storied, labyrinthian home, a place of dark-paneled rooms high brooding ceilings and woodwork heavily, remorselessly varnished, in which she could see her face when she knelt, staring into it. As a child. A child in one of the downstairs parlors, a child in the bedroom with a ceiling that was twelve feet high, too high for a child, and a lovely octagon window she couldn't look out—a child's face framed there, for Jules, in a filmy fading blur of a figure that was almost round, high in air.... *the same face?* No. I've changed a great deal, she said. No. Touching her face, the fingertips cautious and exploratory on the cheekbones where the skin seemed tightest, touching it memorizing it not meaning to say to him *Yes touch me too, touch me like this—lightly— my skin is strange to me, like braille*—He thought he would embrace her, hold her head against him, his chest; but her voice rose from that dark murmur and eased away from him, from them, flying back to that place of hallways like tunnels where there were three fireplaces and the mantels were marble, cool even on the most stale of August days, just the right height for her to press her cheek against.... *You don't hate that place, you don't hate your childhood at all*, Jules said accusingly, and she laughed and said she hadn't hated it, it had hated her, it had expelled her the way your breath is continuously expelling you, breathing you in and then breathing you out, in the same rhythm. Jules stared at her dark, restless blurs of eyes, at the smoky-red mane of hair, the eyebrows wide, unusually wide, but scanty, so that you got the impression of something shadowed there but not precise, and the eyes always moving below the ridge of bone, self-conscious, evasive, alarmed and pleased at being so closely and so lovingly scrutinized....*You were loved there*, Jules said with certainty. *Otherwise, how were you born?...you were loved there and elsewhere too.*

Now her fantasy-face came back. Bantering, coolly bitter, asking him What did he mean love? and making a curious flickering gesture with her fingers which Jules, still a stranger to this part of the continent, could not interpret or see how it might be obscene...though he guessed it was obscene. Yes, there and elsewhere too, she laughed, but here too with you, that's fair for you to say. You make those assessments out of your imagination and I can't get in there to give you a better vocabulary. I saw a rat once...*a what?*...rat, a rat, I saw a rat once, she said, smiling, on a golf course behind the country club, where I was walking one day because one of our homes was....

Was what? Where?

...one of our homes was on a golf course and I used to walk out there, alone, when the weather was too bad for golfers...or at night...and there were ponds there, and marshes, and rats....I saw a rat once attacked by a dog, and the dog was tearing the rat apart and I saw, I saw the eye and behind the eye...the optic nerve...I saw the dog snarling and slashing at the optic nerve....I stood there staring, I couldn't move, I was transfixed. I stood there for a long time. When it was over the dog was gone, the rat was dragged away somewhere, I stood there thinking... and I was thinking of *Yes, what?*...but she looked at him helplessly, Jules now tensed as a guitar string waiting for the touch that would save him, if she would just reach out suddenly to touch him and give him life *Yes, what?*

That I might have to see that again.

Again?

Again and again.

No, no, it's not your seeing that you are seeing, let it go and forget it, Jules murmured, but not loud enough for her to hear. He did not want her to hear. He did not want her to laugh that startled-colt, graceful-mocking laugh of hers, which was so false and which tempted him to hate her.

Again, again, again, she whispered.

On the sixth day, the morning of that day, when he checked his watch eagerly he saw it was 7:25, a sudden leap of his heart roused him from where he slept, fully-clothed, even with his shoes on, to raise himself on one elbow and peer over, yes, yes, there was a movement there, something was happening there, he swung his feet around and grabbed for the field glasses and there she was—a girl drawing the curtains aside at that window at 514 Prince Street, a young woman with a convalescent look about her, the face innocent, wondering, brought up close to Jules' scrutiny like one of his troubled-mumbling dreams...where love with a face like that spoke to him but he lay paralyzed, mute.

He had not expected the movement, the motion of her life, the actual bird-like quality of her presence, *she was not a photograph after all!* and the color of her hair was a shock: not the dark brown he had been told, but a queer reckless slovenly contemptuous mess of colors, dyed black and dyed red, in streaks and strands and glinting patches, very clean, so clean it rose in tiny, almost invisible hairs like a halo about her face, catching the meager sunshine of 7:25 AM and making his eyes water with the strangeness of it....

It was not enough for her to awaken him like this, his heart pounding with the surprise of it, but now, gazing down across the curve of her cheeks into the street...seeing nothing there, nothing that alarmed her...now she tugged at the window, once, twice...the third time she got it up a few inches...*I'll help you!* Jules wanted to cry...and then nearly a foot, and she knelt there, and put her head out the window so that the crazy gleam of black and red soared into Jules' vision, gorgeous hair like a mane, falling so sharply from an irregular part on the right side of her head....She was so close to him that Jules could see the delicate white exposed line of scalp. She leaned out the window, utterly alone. He could see only the top of her head and forehead, she stared down into the street, at a slow-strolling black boy with his hands stuck in his jacket pockets, and when the boy was gone she stared at the sidewalk two storeys below, drawing in long slow wondrous breaths....

For a while they remained like that: Dewalene awakened

from six-days' nightmare, Jules awakened from a sweaty sleep on an army cot. When she raised her head slightly he could see her nostrils darkening, deepening, and then narrowing again, she was forcing herself to breathe through her nose, carefully, deeply. *How near did you come to…?* Don't say it, don't say the word itself, Dewalene whispered. I can think about it and I can accept it, I can inch into it heartbeat by heartbeat, I won't shriek, I won't struggle against it, I know its power over me like the air that was always changing into moisture back where we lived.…You breathe it in with you, it breathes you, I won't kick and thresh and flail my arms around and embarrass everyone, but don't say it, not the word itself. *How long were you unconscious?* O I don't know. *When you took the pills did you think…did you think of how you would wake up and go to the window and lean out and of how I would see you and love you, did you think of anyone, did you think of me, did you see my face?* Nothing. Nothing.

Or if it was a face, why of course it was someone else's.

Someone had once said in Jules' hearing, in a voice he knew well but could not recognize, it was so reverent, so awed, Maybe the child you're supposed to have, the main one, the baby you were born to have, yourself, maybe it's someone you never got around to having…? And he had forgotten the words, had forgotten them completely. But now they came back to him and he heard himself, his own awed interior voice, not the rot-soft hissing voice but another, deeper, brotherly voice, he heard himself saying across the street to a girl roused from the dead and lovely in waking, shaking her long heavy hair out of her eyes and breathing now so he could see her shoulders move, her chest rising and falling: Maybe the one sight you're supposed to have, the main one, the vision you were born to have...maybe it really will come to you, when you've given up...?

How real everything is, how violently we all exist!

But he didn't say that to Ganzfeld, whom he telephoned at once. He dialed 253-4232 but this time the phone was answered by a child, it sounded like a child, saying in amazement...*yeh?* and Jules heard a radio in the background, an announcer's morning-dramatic voice saying It's seven-thirty and time for the weather-report area and national— The receiver must have been snatched out of the child's hand because the next voice was a woman's, asking what did he want? who was it? Jules asked for Mr. Ganzfeld, standing there still excited though the girl was gone now from her window, and the woman yelled *Herb! Herb!* Jules thought it strange, that Ganzfeld should have his office in his home; then he thought that maybe Ganzfeld did not have any office but met people on street corners. It took some time for Ganzfeld to come to the phone.

Yes, what is it?

This is Jules—

What, who? What do you want? It's seven in the morning—

I saw her. I saw the girl.

Look, who is this?

This is Jules on Prince Street—you know—you must remember—

Prince Street what? What the hell? What girl?

The girl at 514 Prince Street—you—know

I got in at four AM and now I'm on the telephone with somebody I don't know and can't even hear distinctly, will you please speak up?—and I'll put on the tape here, O.K., it's being recorded, just say what you've got to say in to it, give your report speaking slowly and distinctly…enunciate each syllable of each word, please.

Get out of the kitchen, your father's busy! someone cried.

There isn't any report, Jules said, nothing happened except I saw her. She opened the window.

Who is this, exactly?—the name?

This is Jules, I'm at 511 Prince Street—

Who? That's "S. Alkon" over there, isn't it?—what happened to him?

To who?

"S. Alkon." *Alkon.* What happened to him?

I thought that was a name, Jules said irritably.

Name!

I just wanted to telephone you to say—

I haven't heard from Alkon for a week. What's going on over there?

Not a week, not that long, Jules said, it's only been six days. I've kept track. I'm calling you because I saw her this morning, a few minutes ago, so there really is someone in there and it isn't a trick of some kind—I mean—you said you thought it might be—a trick some other investigation agency was playing on you—

What's all this? What is this, that you should talk so openly on the telephone, waking me up at six in the morning to a fake report, nothing for Christ's sweet sake to report except you *saw somebody open a window!* Look, you little bastard, I don't know who you are or what game you're playing, but you've been off the payroll since Tuesday, that is, yesterday, so lock up there and leave the equipment in the room, just lock up there and I'll give you the instructions for what to do with the key....

What do you mean, off the payroll? Jules said.

It's ended! It's over! I got word yesterday to drop it, drop her, it's completed, it's a closed book, and where you fit in I don't know—I barely remember you and now an entirely new turn in my life has emerged—I am being retained by a party with a complicated and challenging custody case to win for his client, and as for the past, well, let the dead bury the dead...is she dead?

Look, Jules said, what's going on here?

She's dead?...what did you say a few minutes ago?

I said I saw her, the girl in the room...you know, the photograph?...the girl you said was named Dewalene...? I asked you who she was but you didn't know—

I didn't know? Ganzfeld said angrily. What are you accusing me of? Not knowing what my own work is? who these people are? I make it my business, you smart-mouthed son of a bitch, to know *exactly* what I'm doing, what my position in these cases is, and it seems to me that temporary help like yourself had better watch out!...especially if an assignment, a poor crippled old lady in a wheel chair, with a houseful of Siamese cats and bird-cages in every room, a lovely wealthy old ex-movie-star victim like that, if she should be beaten to death under the surveillance of someone like yourself, probably with a prison record—

What are you talking about? Jules asked.

What are you talking about?

What old lady, what lady in a wheel chair? I don't know any old lady, Jules said. I'm down here on Prince Street. You promised me $4 an hour for keeping a certain person under surveillance, but not an old woman—a girl—a girl, don't you remember? I don't know about any woman in a wheel chair, Jules said....Did someone kill an old woman in a wheel chair?

Let me wake up a little more, Jesus, it's the crack of dawn here, Ganzfeld muttered. *—then turn off that thing!* a woman said. Ganzfeld said, evidently to her and not to Jules, that she should mind her own business; anyway a tape could be erased easily, it did not cost money to record all the conversations, that was the only prudent method....

You gave me the key to 511 Prince Street and you gave me a pair of binoculars and a work-sheet, Jules said hurriedly, and I was to keep under surveillance a certain girl, a young woman named Dewalene...and I was to be paid $4 an hour...you gave me $50 in advance....

Yes, yes, Ganzfeld said groggily. Yes. The girl. That girl.

Yes....Did you say she was a model, or connected with one of the studios? I never got clear on that.

I—

Or was it a divorce case, the husband is trying to prove lewd and lascivious behavior? No! No, that was someone else, weeks ago. Please excuse me. I'm fifty-three years old and the hours are getting me down, wearing me down ....In this particular case, yes I now remember, yes, the husband or whoever it was...I doubt it was a husband, frankly...though maybe it was a husband and the connection with the other people...you know...the connection with the other people is only a coincidence, I don't know and I don't want to know. With such girls there are sometimes husbands, and sometimes ex-husbands, and sometimes husbands-to-be, and they're all jumbled together, I keep files and if you go back for ten, twelve years...ten, twelve years of it...before that I was a sergeant downtown, and got the raw end of a very nasty deal when some smart-ass young lawyer in the DA's office, thinking to climb up there on the corpses of men like myself, twenty-year men like myself, tightened the screws on the whole downtown... but...if you cast your mind back that far you'll see the husbands and the ex-husbands and the future husbands all mixed together in the files, the names you got to cross out and reword they don't know themselves who the hell they are or what they're doing, who they are married to or trying to get divorced from, it's like an octopus in this city. And for $3000 they expect you to erase entire people! But whoever it was, and I did not of course communicate directly with this individual, but with an agent retained by him, and I know from the funny tone of my communicant's voice that *he* did not know who he was acting as agent for...frankly, we all read the newspapers and we can read, we aren't woolly-haired wetbacks up here for a free ride and never bothered to learn the English language except to sign the welfare and ADC checks, if you get my meaning...well, we can all read but my colleague said, he said, Frankly, Herb, I'm all mixed up on this one. So I pass that advice along to you, Jules.

What does that mean?

It means leave the binoculars there and no cigarettes burning or anything, and no light burning, and pull the shade down halfway like it was when you came in, and—

But I just saw her! Doesn't that mean anything? Isn't that important? Jules cried....Don't you *care*?

It's shifted out of my sphere of responsibility, Ganzfeld said. But thank you for wanting to make me feel better, for letting me know—though I already knew, of course—that it wasn't a trick or a scheme to run me ragged and throw my accounts off-balance again. That was thoughtful of you, now that I think of it....Maybe I can use your services again sometime, Jules. I'll be in touch.

Jules did not answer; he stared out into the street. He had the strange idea, the certainty, that the girl was about to appear down there...about to open the front door....

...my nerves are shot these days, Ganzfeld was saying... coffee hypes me up but so goddam it does tea also...which you would expect to be soothing....I'm only fifty-three years old but I have the soul and liver of an eighty-year-old man, no doctor has to diagram it for me. And not from raucous living, either, but from sheer hard work. From keeping pace with this system. All I ever wanted, all I ever made a serious claim to, Jules, was a fair share of everything, a piece of the collective gross national income, and look!... You're a lot younger than I am so maybe you can figure things out—

Yes, yes, Jules muttered, not listening.

—simple question: when this city turns into, as it evidently is, when it collapses into a cesspool where the lowest elements are running it all, where the Mayor is scared shitless by some nigger teenagers and the rest of them are pushing us off the sidewalk, not to mention taxing our life's-blood for their picnic programs and meth heads and retardees and before you know it one day they'll close off the freeways so the city will belong to *them*... when that happens, the morning that happens, you can just say that Herb Ganzfeld predicted it. All of it.

All right, Mr. Ganzfeld.

Yes, and let me bring in a personal note to this, because I am by no means a solitary voice in the wilderness, Ganzfeld said urgently, a friend of mine who runs a window-washing business, just a small modest unpretentious business, this friend of mine my own age and also an ex-policeman, he asks the simple question but the Common Council and the Governor's smart-mouth committee, they don't dare answer him: If citizens don't want niggers washing their windows and staring into their private bedrooms, if they just naturally shy away from the opportunity to be scared shitless by a gang of niggers hoisting themselves up and down the sides of a building, and one of them came on the job already drunk, you might have read about this, Jules, showed up cross-eyed drunk and hoisted himself up to the top of the Charterhouse Inn, which is twenty goddam floors, and then one side of the platform tilted and he fell and grabbed onto the edge of it and was dangling there by one hand in broad daylight, and the whole street gone wild with the spectacle…the fire trucks could hardly get through the crowd.…My friend addresses this simple question to the commission on discrimination: If the client doesn't want this going on outside his windows day after fucking day, doesn't the client have some law on his side…? some *moral law*…

Why

he has to ask, *Why so barbarous*? Running in panic, in perpetual paralyzed flight, he stares up at the ceiling of this place he is in, newly drained of his warm sweet blood and filled with a solution that fizzes in his veins, *Why the questions that must be answered yes*…? For Jules has not been told, and yet he knows very well, that he must say Yes. Yes. Everywhere around him people are moaning, last-minute emergency deliveries are crying No, No, No, don't, No I won't, No I can't, No I never will, but Jules knows that all this is civilization, a mouth up on a stalk mouthing No, No, and it is the wrong word. But why, why is it so barbarous, why is it this noisy isolation when he had hoped only for quiet, for nothing?

All right, Mr. Ganzfeld, he had said, already flying down the stairs and out onto the street, where she was walking—unshaky at first, as if the momentum of the stairs in that building across the way had helped her also. It was a fairly mild day but she wore a coat and her hair was hidden beneath a kind of hood, or a knitted cap that hid the bulky knot of her hair—it must have been pinned up at the back of her head—and Jules took a kind of pride, a premature pride, in the way she headed uphill, up the incline to a wide, loud, busy thoroughfare; there she paused, however, and waited. The cap was dark green. Jules paused a half-block behind her and stared at it, fixing it in his vision.

She stood there so long, he knew something was wrong: she was not going to make it this time. The traffic light changed from red to green to yellow to red again, and the girl stood there, immobile, though he thought he could see her shoulders give way an inch or so, her posture weakened, she was about to turn around and Jules stepped back out of the way, wondering why he should fear her. *Did you know I was there, even then*…? but no, she could not have guessed, every flicker of movement in the city was a threat to her, how to distinguish Jules from the rest of them?

Even with her hair hidden like that she looked a little savage, exaggerated, a hunted creature with its intelligence all forced into cunning and centered in the eyes. Why, Jules wondered, when they were such beautiful eyes?—and later he asked her *Why so barbarous?* Haltingly she asked him, Do you mean me? Or all women?

You and all women.

...speaking seriously, sadly, she told him about other creatures, other animals, how all living things had to endure their freakishness, what caused them to survive but also to declare themselves against the landscape....*It is our nature.* And then he realized that she was talking this way in order to make him curious about her background: describing a thirty-room house she had evidently lived in, for at least part of the year, in a place Jules guessed might be one of those islands off-shore from Oregon or Washington....She said, What looks barbarous to you might be very natural, you have to realize what the barbarity is in response to, and at that moment her thick wavy hair seemed to him as pathetic and reckless as it had looked at first, though her face was serious. What looks savage is almost never savage, she said. What about beauty? Jules wanted to know....She told him about a day she had spent watching wild ducks at the shore, watching the bright green heads of the mallards, staring at them for long minutes at a time...a dozen or more males sitting on the sand amid humps of rock or earth or sand, and then suddenly everything changed: all the birds came to life, the ducks flew away, loosely paired, the brown humps came to life as she stared, and flew as powerfully and urgently as the bright-headed males.... Jules did not understand this. Dewalene said, O you don't see?...it means that the male can die at any time, the male is not needed for very long. In that species the female must be valued, so she is colorless, but the male is plumed and lovely and can die....

Nature makes no mistakes.

Is that really — it? Is that really the reason? And Jules felt the fear of his own recognition; his sorrow for the species to which Dewalene belonged. He said, *Then don't be barbarous, don't be so beautiful, don't be what gets murdered because it's so striking, there, against its environment —*

It's our nature, Dewalene said.

For a while he had followed her, his body effortless with following, with drawing upon her from a half-block, a quarter-block, the fronts of stores and the street traffic and the shapes of other people unclear to him, like the blurry background of a photograph, thinking *I can protect you too, it won't be just what I want you to do*. He felt his expression tighten, concentrated painfully, his gaze narrowed with lust but also with pity—there the girl went into a grocery store, hesitantly, there she walked slowly along the aisles with her head held rigid as if she feared to look from side to side, feared the multitude of cartons and cans and their meanings. Finally she did buy something. Jules waited outside, not wanting her to notice him, and when she came out again he allowed her to walk past him, now in a hurry, back to her apartment.

His throat seemed to thicken with blood, with warm blood. That whisper of his own names, those quickening stabs of lust made him angry, and he had a need to walk faster, to catch up to her. But he wanted at the same time to forget about this, because it was senseless; he wanted to forget about her, to let her go. Several times in his life he had known he was making a mistake, and part of his mind had stood aside, watching silently, as he drifted into the mistake....But he could not judge now: a mistake or not? Needing to get to her and to actually touch her, to let her know that he existed—that might be enough to end it, to release him. He feared losing her, because he might remember her. *To get it over with, to have it done!* He fell into step with her, the same pace, *Who must be murdered?* on a picket sign, and the girl now crossing the street to avoid a small crowd, pedestrians and construction workers from a nearby site arguing with the pickets, Jules staring at her, his motion matched with hers so that even the hesitancy, the vagueness, the occasional stumbling was his. A policeman parked his motorcycle at the curb and Jules glanced nervously at him, not liking policemen, but the man was not interested in Jules at all....Ahead, pausing, staring back at the crowd in front of the courthouse, Dewalene stood with the grocery bag in her arms, held against her chest, and the green-knit cap slid down slowly to show her hair; she didn't seem to be aware of it. She stood for a while, like that, so that Jules had to stop to wait, wait eagerly, pretending to stare into a shop window...in which he saw after a few seconds his own shadowy reflection...but distorted, dim, not showing the full color of his heated face.

Now a few yards between them, now only a few feet, now he sees how she is aware of him—glancing at him—breathing through her parted lips, very frightened. She has stopped in front of a shoe store. *Hedy's Shoes.* Her head is bare today, and the black-red hair falls down loosely, untidily. Her complexion is sickly. It has been nine days since Jules first stared across the abyss of Prince Street, and now on the ninth day, right now, he is going to touch her. There is a bin of bargain shoes here, heaped-up shoes with their straps tangled together, sandals and heavy club-sized square-toed shoes, ballet slippers, even boots, even rhinestone-studded shoes, and the girl stands there, staring down at these shoes, her face paralyzed in a kind of half-smile, her gaze inward and blind. She is wearing a dress that looks too big for her, loose at the hips, even falling oddly from her shoulders…and her feet, Jules sees, are bluish-white, naked inside the rundown sandals she is wearing. He notices that the back of each heel is slightly reddened, from the straps. *I wanted to kneel down and kiss you there!* He edges up to her, himself nervous and cold at his fingertips. *I wanted to walk away, I wanted to cross the street and walk away.* …But he didn't know: was there a steady relentless wind blowing him into his future, his own being, and was this wind almost tangible about him, currents of ordinary city air charged and trembling? Later he would want to tell her, *There's another wind blowing us backward to forget, back into the past before we were born, into a reservoir of pastness in which even beauty like yours can't be distinguished from the rocks that line this continent and hint to us of things we don't want to name….*

So he stands there, between the two rhythms, the two heartbeats.

❖

She was very frightened. He believed he could smell the panic in her. And he was going to edge up to her, he was going to say, *I'd like to talk to you don't be afraid it's*, and suddenly she turned to him blinking, as if she were facing a strong light, and she tried to smile, she said something he could not quite hear—

What?

She said, staring at him, You're...? You're the one I...? I'm...?

What do you mean? Jules said, alarmed.

You're the one to drive me up there? she said.

Drive you where?

O out of this, out of the city...aren't you the one? They told me there would be, there would be someone...they said...they. They said someone would help me...?

Jules was astonished.

...someone would help...? Because it's been a long time ...and nobody came...and I....

Where did you want to go? Jules said.

She shook her head slowly. She said, But aren't you the person who was supposed to meet me? Or are you someone else...? I saw you the other day, I saw you out on the street ....You must be that person. You are, aren't you?

She smiled. She touched his arm. She said, You know my name, don't you?—you know me, don't you?

I do know you, Jules said, *but*—

Do you know my name?

Yes, but—

What is it?

Dewalene, he said.

And she closed her eyes with relief; she leaned toward him, weakly. Yes, she said, Yes, yes. Yes. Good. Yes, that's it. *Because it wasn't your name?* That's the right name, that's the name, yes, she said, yes…Dewalene.

Dewalene.

But she wasn't weak, she wasn't so precarious. Half-formed then, she took shape for him later, and he began to feel the impact of her fierce, sweet beauty, when he tried to make out who she was and what was happening, what she wanted from him except a ride up the coast, and she stood in the center of that room at 514 Prince Street and smiled at him, smiling I'm sorry, I'm sorry, none of that concerns you, I won't tell you.

Jules scratched his head.

I can't drive. I'm terrified of driving, she said. I've been through….I haven't been well. I don't mean now, the last few days…I mean…before this, a while before this….And I don't have a driver's license.

He asked her if she had had one before…?

Before what? she asked, smiling. But her voice showed irritation.

Jules indicated the room: *This.*

You mean my having come down so low? you mean the mess in here, the smell…? It smells of sickness, of something sick, yes, I realize that, I have been sick, but now I'm well. Now you're here to help me. Aren't you? And I've been well for several days…I admit that I, I made some mistakes in my life...I....But I've been well for several days. It seemed to come back to me....

She smiled, wanting him to smile. *Life came back to you...*?

Yes. It did. I was very disturbed about something, you might know what it is...do you? Did they tell you?

No.

I was disturbed, I was not really in my own mind, in my own soul. I made some mistakes beginning about a year and a half ago....They have to do with people. Certain people. One man in particular...but....But all that's over now. I went away by myself, to be alone and away from certain influences...and...and those influences followed me, they seemed to be in waiting for me in my sleep. They got the better of me for a while. I was terrified of sleep, of falling asleep...because....

Yes, Jules wanted to say, yes. Yes.

...because a certain person would come to me then....I don't believe in him any longer, I don't believe in the power people claim over others, I really don't believe it, she said. She stood facing Jules, her arms folded. He could imagine her strong, fierce, defiant—a precocious-child daring to her, an air just in the way she smiled at him of her knowing secrets he would never know. *Spoiled little bitch.* And it hit him then that she was not helpless but superior to him: that she had assumed almost immediately her own superiority, but not consciously, not deliberately. She must have been born to this, Jules thought, annoyed; ordering people around.

No, she said, seriously, no, I don't believe in it—the power people claim over others. It isn't real. It's just….

Jules looked skeptical. What power? What people? He wondered if she was talking this way, so emphatically, to confuse him all the more. She warmed to that look of his, however, nodding as if he were helping her in this—even relaxing, letting her arms fall at her sides, letting go—saying, Yes, you agree with me? You do, don't you? That there isn't this…this influence of one mind over another…?

I don't know, Jules said. He glanced around the room—taking in only the plainness of it, the anonymous pale-yellow walls, the total lack of mystery in this place he had so violently imagined—and away from her intense, staring face. She wanted him to agree with her but he didn't know what she was talking about, and he sensed her knowing this —his own befuddlement—but not caring, so desperate was she to be convinced. He said that he would drive her where she wanted to go: he would be happy to. He would help her. But he wanted to know a little more of….

You already know, Dewalene said.

I don't, Jules said.

You already know as much as anyone does, she said, and anyway it's better not to know too much about him. That was where I went wrong, getting too close…I drifted into it, I didn't know what would happen….I'm not that young, she said, laughing, I mean I'm no longer seventeen years old, the way some of them are: when I was seventeen I still lived at home. But now they get younger and younger….I'm twenty-three. I'm really not very young, not by California standards…for this sort of thing…I mean…you know what I mean, don't you?

Generally, Jules said. *I suppose so*.

And I did it against my own nature, she said, to punish myself. I did it deliberately. I mean at first, deliberately, choosing a way to descend that was disgusting to me, because I wanted to shake up my life, my personality…I wanted to get outside of myself, outside of my selfish life, I'd been hypnotized into it.…But beyond a certain point I lost control. I couldn't choose any longer. I was living for a while with…with some people…and I lost track of time, and things happened during those times, that come back to me now. They come back in flashes. But what I want to explain to you is…is that the nightmares are over, I think, and the hallucinations in the air…and…and I don't think I'll ever try that again, what I tried a few days ago. Dosing my system like that. I won't ever do that again. Because it was like a miracle, I came back to life…I had to get to the window and put my head out, and breathe the air…I had no control over it, something just came into me and through me, like electricity, calling my name and crying: Get up! Get up!…And so I dragged myself over there, over to the window.…

That window, that one…? Jules asked.

…yes, that one. I dragged myself over there. And it seemed to me that the nightmares were ended, that I had come through. I don't know why. I don't deserve it.

She seized her long thick hair in both hands and smoothed it back from her face, back and down, eagerly, swiftly, girlishly, saying to Jules that the very air had changed, the taste of the air had changed, something had passed by her and left her untouched and now she didn't want to die, after all, because the memories would fade, she was sure they would fade, and she would forget. And she would begin over again somewhere else.

Back home? Jules asked.

Home where? she asked.

She was moving around the bed, pulling the bedclothes up. She made the bed quickly, hurriedly, kept getting the cover too long on one side and then on the other, self-conscious as Jules watched her, yet finicky and arrogant too. She glanced at him over her shoulder, saying, Home where?...You don't know anything about my home. Whether I have a home or not.

Her legs showed muscle at the calf, strong legs, though quite pale—a pallor worse than her face—almost dead-white, as if she had been hidden away from the sunshine for some time. Tiny blue veins at the back of the knees, and the toes rather long, narrow, the big toe especially long, the toenails grown out too long, so that it passed through Jules' mind whimsically—he even smiled—that he must be careful of those toenails or they'd scrape his legs raw. And glancing up at her he couldn't keep that look off his face: sheer calculating desire. But Dewalene was too nervously absorbed in making the bed to notice this; she was still talking to him, at him, as if giving directions—

The drive will take only two days and they'll pay you, where we're going. Please trust me. I assume they gave you an advance—

Jules shrugged his shoulders.

—and at the other end you'll get the rest. I don't even know, she said cheerfully, what they're giving you…I don't know about such things, such arrangements.

Don't you?

It's only such a relief to me to get out of here, out of this, she said. A while ago I wanted to die, I did want to die…but then it passed through me, as if part of me did die, and what stayed living is very…well, very happy now.…I'm so grateful to you, I'm grateful you're the one to help me. Because you seem like a nice person.…

She laughed, embarrassed. Her face colored.

Now don't patronize me, Jules said meanly.

O I'm not! I'm not!

He was flattered by her confusion.

I didn't mean to patronize you, she said slowly. Not me, not of all people me.…I have no right to patronize anyone.

That private, anguished pallor of hers! Almost, Jules wanted to look away; it was disturbing to him, obscene. Though he knew nothing about her he seemed suddenly to know everything. He seemed to be looking into her, into her wide self-hating vacant stare, and he felt a kinship with her self-hate: a knowledge of her, as if he had penetrated her body with his own. He knew his mind was making wrong turns, wrong decisions. It was making him stand here, taking orders from a stranger, a girl who was hectic and highly-charged and too intense for him, even if she weren't soiled by near death and by his own fantasies of the two of them threshing on the floor here together.…It was making him hectic himself, with a lovely false rosiness, a springing-up of excitement he knew was somehow morbid. She apologized again, in that slow and rather formal voice, making an issue of it...patronizing him even now, with her apology. You see how polite I am, even to someone like you.

No, he wouldn't love her. He wouldn't even make love to her. No, Jules thought, not this time.

...never meant to insult you, my God, I owe my very life to you, she was saying, I have no one but you to get me out of here.

He waited half an hour for Ganzfeld, his mind beating angrily. Where was that bastard, what was wrong, what was this, who did Ganzfeld think he was...? Jules was dizzy with the impact of Dewalene, stronger now than when he had actually been with her: out on the street here, waiting at an intersection, he saw the ordinary faces of people about him, men and women, sexless neutral uncharged faces, saw how flat they were and how disappointing.... None of them Dewalene, none of them arrogant and helpless! He felt almost a kind of nausea, a helplessness of his own, to realize that something had opened up in him, a secret craving, and that no one could satisfy it but Dewalene; that, somehow, without quite knowing it, he had delivered himself over to her. By the time Ganzfeld showed up Jules had become quite impatient.

....you? Ganzfeld asked, surprised.

Jules turned. There he was, looking worse than ever:

unshaven, anxious, rumpled. His hair was combed oddly, in a way Jules did not recall, long thin wet-looking strands combed over the crown of his head. Was this Ganzfeld?

You look angry about something, Ganzfeld said.

The voice was the voice on the telephone: so it must have been Ganzfeld.

Jules ignored this and handed the key over to Ganzfeld, as if this were a very important transaction, done in silence, Jules frowning and the two of them drawn close together— with a mechanical, perfunctory intimacy that might have meant they were old friends, accustomed to dealing with each other on a busy street corner at 10 PM. Ganzfeld slapped his pockets, whistled relief—almost forgot the money, ha ha—and handed Jules an envelope and Jules pocketed it without checking it, being an associate of Ganzfeld's and not suspicious of anything. Jules asked if he wanted the photograph back…?

Of the girl? Ganzfeld laughed. Christ no.

Jules raised his eyebrows.

Oh yeh, a funny thing, Ganzfeld said, drawing near to Jules again as if to tell him a joke, and hearty with him now that their relationship was finished, you know my wife…you know how superstitious she is…well, it turns out she had a dream about that girl! All along!

What do you mean, all along? Jules asked.

Ganzfeld mumbled something about his wife's dreams— premonitions—and seemed to be imitating her, or at any rate altering his voice a little and twisting his expression around—not that *he* was superstitious!—though Jules didn't think that was a very good imitation of the man's wife, and stood unsmiling, waiting for it to come to an end. Vaguely, remotely, he knew that something was wrong. He waited for Ganzfeld to complete the dream.

...always worries about me, you know how women are. I try to explain to her, well, it was worse when I was on the force: the niggers are apt'a run right in with shotguns these days, to liberate their brothers from the jail-block.... Ganzfeld shook his head. He went on to tell Jules that he had enjoyed their association and would certainly call on Jules again: the Star Hotel, right? and explained in a rush how perfect Jules had been for the job, how certain he, Ganzfeld, had been as soon as they met, after a morning and an early afternoon of spies from other agencies, sons of bitches sent out to sabotage Ganzfeld's career....It's a difficult life, Ganzfeld sighed, but a challenging one. Ah well....

Jules thought he might leave now: he smiled and backed away. He could not resist *She is a very beautiful girl, that Dewalene....*

Ganzfeld gaped at him.

Is...?

Not to exaggerate, not to exaggerate, not humanity or himself or god-gluttonous events that link them, but his body was exaggerated and stiff with misery. He could not believe that she was doing this: turned away from him swiftly, indifferently like a sister pulling something over her head, something to sleep in, and then shyly slipping the dress down past her hips, stepping out of it barefoot....

O I'm so tired suddenly, suddenly exhausted, she whispered, and it was true how wasted she looked. Even her ferocious hair looked spent in wide wavy strands. Jules stooped to pick a hair up: long, glinting black. A single hair. Watching her, covertly, his lust making him angry, he wound the hair around his left thumb and listened to her rapid murmur which was like a farewell, backing away and eyes averted out of alarm at seeing a stranger in this room with her:...have a gun? If you do, please don't show it to me. I don't want to know about it. I would rather not know... who you are or what your reasons are for being involved in this....

Jules said nothing. He went to the window facing the street, thinking suddenly that maybe someone could see in...Dewalene had not bothered to draw the blind down to the window sill...only the curtains were closed, yanked together, dust-weary white curtains with ruffles. Jules stared out to the building across the way. *There, that room.* He looked across to the window of that room, S. Alkon's room, and it seemed to him innocent enough...opaque with darkness. Was someone inside? Jules scanned the front of the building, the rows of windows, far to the left and then down again and back around and up again, past the window he had gazed out for so many long hours, and all this told him nothing. Most of the windows were illuminated, shades were drawn carefully, a few of the windows showed only darkness inside: Was someone watching?

Jules turned around and she was staring at him. Is something wrong? she said. What are you looking at...?

He pulled the blind down.

…this is a quiet neighborhood, Dewalene said quickly, because of the factories over there, I mean, they don't seem to be operating at full capacity, at least not at night …so it's quiet around here, in the street, isn't it? I don't think there is anyone out there….

Jules said there was no one out there: No.

…the only people who know where I am are people who want to help me, Dewalene said. She was wearing a thing that came to her knees, unevenly, a pull-over tunic or shift of a very thin jersey material; she folded her arms, as if she were cold, but really to hide her breasts from him—though she did this unconsciously, smiling at him and telling him, insisting that there was no danger any longer and never had been, No, the only danger was in my imagination, she laughed, because I exaggerated so much….

Jules said ironically: *Yes. Sure.*

She went to the bed and pulled the covers back and got in, facing the wall. He thought she looked like a mechanical doll, getting into a bed without looking at the bed. They lay there, motionless. Razor-sharp his gaze went, very cruel, his lips lifting from his teeth to say something cruel….*No danger, no, of course not, no danger, none at all!* But he forced his voice to be gentle, to sound gentle. He said, *All right, go to sleep if you can, nothing will happen and we'll leave around six….All right?*

She made a sound that meant yes, all breath, a child's sweet brainless sigh.

…then lifting her head she whispered, About the gun…?

Jules had turned off the overhead light. The room was fairly dark.

...if you have one, if you have one, Dewalene said quickly, please don't use it? Don't use it?

Why would I have to use it, since there's no danger involved in this?

It's true there is no danger, I mean the only danger is... was...in my imagination, in my nightmares, Dewalene said, because people can't have influence over others... they can't control them across distances...no, there's no danger and no need for a gun, maybe you should leave it behind. Jules? Maybe you should leave it behind.

All right, I'll leave it behind.

...you're so strange, so nice, you do whatever I ask, Dewalene said. But don't watch me now, please. I'm so tired....My head feels so heavy, she said laughing, letting it fall onto the pillow, it feels the way it might feel on the planet Jupiter....Yes, she said, softly, as if drifting into sleep or pretending, yes, you're strange, you're not like me. You're the opposite of me, Jules.

Am I?

Yes. Because I came into this, I came down into this, of my own free will....But I don't think you did. I think you're just here, with me tonight, watching over me tonight... you're just here in this part of the world by accident...and anywhere you would be, it would be by accident....

Don't patronize me, Jules wanted to say lightly. But it stung him: the truth of what she said.

...accidental, innocent, a second-and-a-half of absolute

pure light shone into the brain, then the rushing-in of the world again, never pulverized down to nothing. *Don't patronize me, please*, Jules says, though he knows himself a criminal and a murderer—and when he mumbled a delirious confession to murder, once, coming out of the anesthesia after an emergency operation in 1972, in some post-operative room cold and silent as an incubator for creatures without blood, crying out that confession he half-knew half-dreaded he would cry out, if consciousness ever deserted him in any institution in which the staff wore uniforms—what did it matter? what did the delirium matter? any more than the murder itself, the struggle with a policeman in broken glass and flowers and air stinking from a broken refrigeration unit? *I killed a man*, Jules had wept, *I shot him in the face— Do something with me, help me, put me away, obliterate me*—rising rocking from side to side groggy and sick, deathly sick, sick with the profound dead-end-blank sickness of the moon seen upside-down and inside-out from that street near the beach where he lay, having been dragged out of his taxi and beaten savagely in the face, his nose broken, his eyes hammered shut except for slits through which to view the moon, and something terrible stuffed down his throat—oh Christ what had they done to him, those black boys?—Jules who meant no harm, who meant only to make a living and see what this edge of the continent would reveal to him— something metallic and columnar like a flashlight shoved down his throat and meant to kill him—Out of delicacy or because no one knew or remembered, the exact nature of that object was never revealed to Jules. He had gasped his way up through the suffocation and the whining of sirens and the sudden jump of time to waking, recovering, weeping that confession, into the not-very-wakeful face of a man who looked too young to be a doctor but must have been a doctor, saying *O Christ I killed a man once, back home, it was a cop, a stranger*, and the face above him wobbled and teased him because it wouldn't give him any sign: Yes? No? And finally he woke and the intern was saying,...you're the third one this week, and Jules asked out of a mist of pain,...*third one what?* O to confess to a cop-killing, said the intern blandly, and Jules fell back and lay there and sleepless his soul throbbed with *Don't patronize me! Don't!*

...which they don't, any longer.

Because they don't seem to see him: he doesn't exist.

Dewalene lies beside me and her face is close to mine. It is not quite a formed face, not quite permanent....in the making, it must be kissed into shape, kneaded carefully and gently into its true shape...and for this I was born, I, and no one else, I, Jules, whether I exist or not or she exists, whether her name was that name or the other name she finally told me, or no name at all, whether it was all a lie, a phantasmagoria, whether everything is a lie or a phantasmagoria, we are the same substance and love each other here, in it, kissing each other's faces into shape. For this we are born, for the gentle breathing between us, and Dewalene rises above me and kisses me with that strange, inquisitive mouth, the lips tense at first and then softening, softening, I can feel the smile of her lips, the muscular precision of a smile....*Jules, are you dreaming? Again?*...she kisses me through the dreaming, through the sweet hypnotic certainty of dreaming, as if pursuing me, she is so sweet, so secret, I can feel the kisses now forming inside her before they are pressed onto my face....Those kisses are Dewalene herself, the formless forming of her soul, which eases into my soul like an extension of her kiss, her caressing, her love. For this Dewalene was born. Her breath is like mine and my slightly accelerated heartbeat is hers, a beat that goes through us, a powerful inaudible throbbing like the crashing of waves on the beach when we are there to hear it and when we are not there ....*You love me*, she whispers, and then corrects herself *You loved me.*

Abruptly, the photograph and the headline came into focus and Jules stood there shocked more by the girl's smile and her plump childish face than by the headline in red letters DARLENE TELLS OF HER NIGHTMARE NIGHT and in black letters more modestly beneath that LONE STEWARDESS-SURVIVOR OF SEX MANIAC'S ORGY, 4 BUNGALOW-MATES SLAIN, then the black attendant had driven up and was saying something about the tank being nearly full, and the oil O.K., and it's good luck the battery isn't dead, after so long. Jules looked away from the tabloid paper lying there in the booth. The black man's tone had already surprised him, being so respectful; and now the man was handing him the keys to a car—a low-slung powder-blue car of some foreign manufacture, bizarre in its lines, cruelly angular, obviously very costly—Jules just stared at it, as the attendant chattered of how the garage here had two other Jaguars and they were his first choice of a car, of all the cars though there was a $50,000 car on the premises also, parked more or less permanently on the sixth level, a Rolls-Royce convertible owned by....

Thank you, Jules said.

At the top of the ramp it stalled and the attendant called out, Use the clutch!—the clutch! and Jules sweated and waved back at him, Thank you, and got the car going very slowly, painfully, and out on the street it stalled again, a red light flashed on, and he shut everything off and sat there smelling the leather upholstery and the early-dawn damp and another, fainter, less personal odor than the slept-in clothes he was wearing and hadn't changed for all he could remember in his recent life. A man in a trench coat, cheerful, clean-shaven, came over to the curb and startled Jules, leaning down to give him advice:...pump the gas pedal three times, yes, very slowly, you must pamper it, yes, like that, now the clutch...now turn on the ignition, but be careful to....

Thank you, Jules said.

When Dewalene came out, carrying her suitcase and a leather purse with a broken strap and her coat slung over one arm, she stared at the car and smiled strangely, and told Jules it didn't exactly look familiar to her: She had not remembered it being so large.

It's the correct car, Jules said. He laughed.

If the keys fit, well then of course it must be the correct car, Dewalene said. She was putting her things in the back. Her hair brushed against Jules' arm, outstretched on the back of the passenger's seat, and he smelled an early-morning cleanness about her, she woke innocent and evidently rested from a night of teeth-grinding whimpering dreams he would never ask her about, and to make conversation he reported the garage attendant's remarks, *Good luck that the battery is still working*, and asked her casually, *How long has it been since you've driven this car?*

Dewalene had trouble closing the door. The catch didn't seem to take hold.

I've never driven this car, she said.

You never have?

No.

Whose car is it, then?

It's in my name, Dewalene said. She seemed to continue, as if to say, *It must be my car, then*; but she said nothing. She opened the glove compartment. There were several road-maps inside and a pink plastic comb and some wadded-up Kleenex. She couldn't get the door of the glove compartment to stay shut, then, and Jules had to force it into place. She rubbed her fingers together, complaining of how they stung from trying to twist that damn thing, and how she hated cars anyway. Jules asked her if she was ready?—and he reached past her, around her, to slam the door shut on her side.

She flinched.

You look very rested, Jules said to calm her; *you look very healthy now and beautiful. Just tell me where to drive.*

North. North of the city, she said. *But don't take any of the freeways. Please.*

Why not?

I'm afraid of them.

But—

Just drive north…out toward the ocean…and when we're out of the city tell me. And she leaned forward to hide her face against her knees, her hands cupped at the back of her neck.

Are you sick? Jules asked. *What's wrong?*

Just drive. Drive out of here.

Down the five-hundred-foot drop he could see it, falling forward, the distorted front of the car falling, falling forward and down— But he fixed his attention on the road and kept driving.

> north, north of the city
> and out of here

Dewalene seemed to be repeating, but silently. Jules had the strange idea—

No.

—the idea that one of the oncoming cars or one of the cars propelled so recklessly past him was going to—

But no, why should he think that, and a few hours later he stopped at a roadside restaurant near Cayucos Beach and the girl hesitated, then said she'd stay in the car, she felt a little shaky. So Jules went to get something to eat and brought it back to her and they sat there, the door on Jules' side swung open, eating in silence. Dewalene's hands trembled. He saw covertly the trembling paper cup, the coffee swaying inside, thought that she was maybe just hungry—

Why so frightened? Jules asked.

She laughed and said she wasn't frightened, but excited, she'd driven so often along this highway in the past, sometimes alone and sometimes with friends from college, and it was exciting to see how the route was still the same, the places were still the same, nothing had changed, oh yes there was more traffic but not much had changed along the coast—there, there was a quail!—and she pointed at something Jules couldn't see, it must have been too quick for him. Dewalene was saying how strange it was that she was here, safe, sitting here in a car in the parking lot of a restaurant, and across the highway was the drop-off and the ocean, and some chaparral along the edge of the road, it was all what she had remembered and very strange....

Jules wanted to know why it was strange.

...everything the same. The same way. The same way it was. He asked her politely did she want anything more to eat, obviously she was starved, and she said at once No, no thank you, but Jules felt her shakiness, her hunger, so he went back into the restaurant and asked the girl for a few more sandwiches, and to wrap them, please, and when he came back out Dewalene was putting on sunglasses, and through the curved windshield of the car she looked as if she were underwater...the color of her skin slightly sallow, because of the windshield's distortion, the blue-tinted lenses of the glasses queer, deathly, unfriendly. She wrapped the wire earpieces carefully behind her ears.

Out-of-state cars, campers, trailers...small busses... even a converted mail truck with its doors ajar, diapers and towels visible inside, swaying from a clothesline. A long straggling line of bicyclists pedaling laboriously uphill, the one nearest Jules wobbling, *Jesus Christ if he swings that wheel out—* Dewalene kept adjusting the sunglasses on her face, on her nose, Jules nervously watched the road and thought of the cliff, the car end-over-end, how someone was driving down from the north to meet them head-on. *Are you sick? What's wrong?* until the tension made him say *Talk to me, please. Say something.*

How startled she was!—to realize she was being impolite. And she looked at him guiltily, as if really seeing him now, and apologized for being so quiet, she knew it was.... She asked him where he was from, and how did he like it out here? and Jules caught the slight, very slight condescension in her voice, though she was shaky yet and kept staring at him and adjusting the glasses nervously, rubbing at the bridge of her nose. Jules said he was from Detroit, but he didn't want to talk about himself; she asked why and he said he already knew about himself, and none of it was worth knowing, and with her quick instinctive politeness she laughed and said something about how good he had been to her....

Last night, I mean.

Last night when he had let her alone, sitting slouched in a chair and half-sleeping; guarding her without a gun, listening to her breathe so heavily and whimper in her sleep, his mouth twitching ironically to tell him *Jules what the hell is this*, but he had been good to her and he didn't regret it....She began to talk quickly, her voice only going a little vague when someone tried to pass Jules, inching out and inching back, inching out again painfully recklessly around the curves and up and down the hills, sometimes boys in sports cars that roared angrily and sometimes boys on motorcycles, but Jules kept hitting the brakes and wouldn't go any faster...*My real name is Clare*, she said shyly, *I mean on my birth-certificate*.

Yes?

Dewalene is a...a gift. A gifted-name.

For a while Jules said nothing, knowing that if he asked who had gifted her with it she'd turn away, then he said *How long have you had that name?* and she explained that it was very new to her, only a year or eight months ago, she wasn't exactly sure...because time was strange to her.... because the summers here are very long and she was accustomed to more change.

I liked Clare. But.

Dewalene came as a gift, a gift. Afterward, she said, she tried to go back to Clare because she was through with that particular society…that membership….But….

Jules asked her if the person who'd given her the name was the same one who'd given her the car and she laughed and said no, not exactly, no it wasn't, exactly. *But they're all connected. They even answer to the same name, sometimes.*

He glanced over at her and saw her watching him.

Which name was it?

She said nothing for a while. Along the road were hitch-hikers in two's and three's and Dewalene ducked her head slightly, instinctively, without noticing, then put her hand out suddenly onto Jules' arm and said *Up ahead—up ahead there's a turn-off—* She squeezed his arm. *Can you turn off there?—right there—yes, here—*

They spent the afternoon there, until the daylight was gone.

Dewalene in a state of euphoria, clutching at him. It was like rage, lifting and falling and lifting again, her face pale, strained, set. He saw her eyes go blind. All intake of breath, all yearning—she kept murmuring *I love you, I love you*—then saying his name as if it were an incantation, *Jules Jules Jules.* The sound of the ocean came distantly but from all sides. *Jules. Jules.* A long sullen heavy crashing, a rhythmic crashing, two violent substances crashing together, mysteriously, driving him into a frenzy as Dewalene ran her hands slowly over his body, saying *You know you love me, you love me, you know it*, until they lay together stunned with all the noises of the day and the rocking motion of the earth and the incredible, whip-like, stinging need of their bodies to come together.

Then Dewalene shuddered and said, When I saw you out on the street…the first day…I knew who you were but I was afraid, I was afraid of you already…Because I knew this would happen, I couldn't stop it from happening.

Jules embraced her and comforted her, wanting to love her again but weak still from the agony of their soft-fleshed shell-less bodies and those minutes of struggle, the near-weeping, that explosive pleasure….For a while she had been almost uncontrollable. Her face contorted, her breath ragged, her body hot and straining as if with rage….but he wanted to go back to it, to her, to see if it had really happened *You love me, you know it*, how they had struggled in their love, in a beat more violent than any heartbeat….

Something ached in his face, his cheek. He laughed and kissed her. She sat up, let her forehead droop to her knees, her long hair glinting in the sun, and Jules caressed it, caressed her, talking to her….She began to respond to him. She said I knew this would happen, I knew, I went crazy for you just now…I couldn't help it…I can't help it.

Death in small electric leaps, spasms, explosion-by-explosion of brain cells: Jules stroked her and kissed her and smiled into her strained face.

…for the night?

O I don't care, she whispered, *Wherever you want to.*

Will you stay with me?

Yes.

I mean instead of....?

...of going up there to meet them? She looked at him. She reached for the sunglasses, lying on the ground a few feet away. *No, I can't do that. But I can meet you sometime again. Sometime later.*

Where do you have to be tomorrow? —why is it so urgent?

Even now she was in a kind of delirium, though quiet beside him, adjusting the sunglasses again...he felt her mind sway, sway from him and back again...

Jules, she said *I have to be somewhere tomorrow; I can't alter those plans. All this is to protect me...or it was to protect me, because I don't really think I'm in danger. Somehow I think it's gone now. I think...I think it's gone now.*

They were sitting in a kind of ravine, a dry gulch, a few hundred yards from the highway. The sky was very blue. From somewhere behind them came two soft, guttural notes, and Dewalene turned to look...her hair brushing against Jules' face....*I love birds, I love animals*, she whispered, *when I was a girl and...* She talked for a while about a house her family had had, somewhere north of here, and the birds she had been able to watch from the window of her room: sparrow hawks, jays, quails, red-winged blackbirds, gulls, geese of all kinds, and her eyes behind the cool blue-tinted lenses avoided his while she talked and he caressed her arm, slowly, caressing her to make her more like himself, more physical, more subdued. He helped her to her feet and brushed at her clothing, smiling, trying to joke with her a little, but already he was shy with her—this tall, handsome girl with the bizarre hair, wild as a bird's outlandish crown, her delicate ribs moving beneath the surface of her skin as he touched her, held her, a pulse in her neck moving beneath his lips, warmly and stubbornly as her mind swayed this way, that way....

Suddenly a thought crossed Jules' mind: he seemed to see again the photograph of that stewardess, "Darlene," her pouty smile and the three-inch red headlines, almost dizzily he seemed to see it again, while this girl was telling him, still, in a maddening-slow vague voice, about her childhood and how she had disliked it, how she had been so lonely, and only the birds and the animals and the hope of having friends when the summer was over...only these kept her going...she'd been so lonely, hidden away because her parents were at war, detectives had spied on her, she'd been the center of a custody case and....Jules interrupted her: *That trial back in Los Angeles—does it have anything to do with that?*

Does what? What? What do you mean? she stammered.

Being in danger, being driven up here by me—all this— hiding out the way you were— Are you connected with any of them, the girls who were murdered?

Dewalene said angrily that those girls were airline stewardesses!

He killed other girls too, Jules said. *Didn't he?*

I didn't follow the case, Dewalene said.

I didn't either, said Jules. *But are you related to any of them?—or to him?—or is there any connection?*

As far as I know some man killed some airline stew-ardesses! he was a maniac, Dewalene said. She spoke without looking at Jules. She stepped carefully back down into a level, flattened-out area, where some debris had been strewn and cars had been parked, and Jules followed her, slipping on a loose rock but not falling, staring at her back and the tangled mane of hair, his body still blood-sodden with love, heavy, pleased, perplexed, saying to the girl's stiff back, *You might be mistaken about me, Dewalene*, saying calmly though she did not look around or even hesitate, but continued along the faint trail where the car was parked and the door on Jules' side was swung open into the high grass, *How do you know who I am, exactly? —who I'm working for?*

Dewalene went back to the car and slid in.

Jules' heart was pounding: frustration, anger, disap-pointment, alarm. The girl had taken something out of her purse, was wiping her face with it carefully, her forehead and then her cheeks, dabbing up beneath the sunglasses to get her eyes, as if wiping him off her, rubbing herself clean of him. He stood for a while looking down toward the highway, at the string of cars rising and falling, both lanes crowded, and beyond the highway the ocean—a deep, white-capped blue, the white-caps crashing and dis-appearing and cracking open again as he stared.

Yes Jules, yes, yes I love you, she had moaned, grinding her helpless face against his, but he wondered who *Jules* was and how many other names he had.

…She leaned over to call him, saying he shouldn't be

angry—why be angry?—now smiling, her lips smiling, stretching, and Jules saw with surprise that she had put on lipstick—her face rosy with color, not the face he had loved half an hour before, but very friendly to him, very nice. He came back, they ate the rest of the sandwiches, she sighed and spoke to him again of her childhood and a complicated divorce case and the custody case— "I was famous for having been spied on, constantly, by my own father!" she laughed—and Jules listened to this thinking that it had nothing to do with her, with him, with the two of them or why she was here, that it may have been true—certainly was true—but told him nothing, really. Yet he said nothing; he couldn't accuse her of lying. She leaned her head against his, and then against his shoulder. She put her hand over his, his hand rigidly gripping the steering wheel, and asked him how old he was?—a little surprised that he was ten years older than she was, she would have guessed, oh, he was twenty-eight, no more, then her mind seemed to roam a bit and she asked what religion he was?—and Jules had to laugh at that, it sounded so queer, but he said he'd been Catholic but had drifted out of it, and what about her?—*O nothing, nothing at all*, she said flatly, *but the last year I was at college—I dropped out, my senior year—to go to Veracruz with some people—there was a religious event in my life, and it changed my life—* Jules felt now that she was circling near to what must be said between them, but he showed no curiosity, saying that they should get on the road again and find a motel, he was exhausted, starved, he would like to sleep that night and she should sleep also—and Dewalene kissed him and pressed her face against his, saying, *I think God came to me and it terrified me, I think that caused me to make some errors...I couldn't comprehend it...I ran away from it, from being the person I was, and into other things...into strange things....And....And so I'm here with you. Don't ask me about my life.*

...did you ever meet him?—the murderer?

Oh, him! she said contemptuously, *what about him?—I may have been at some house parties he was invited to—I really don't know—I don't want to talk about it— He isn't important.*

Where were these parties? What kind of parties?

Parties.

What did you mean—God came to you? Is that what you said?

No. I don't know what I said.

What did you just say?

Jules, for Christ's sake—

Yes, for Christ's sake! I'm asking you what you just said! I said I'm here with you, I said don't ask me about my life.

And again that night they loved each other, near enough to the sea to feel the shudder of the waves, trying to beat back the throb of the sea to get everything quiet, subdued. Jules tried to still her, to bring that wildness of hers to a pitch and then ease it down again, feeling his soul cry out with her, expand violently to every part of her threshing body, and then go quiet, still, into peace. But they did not really meet except inside her: and then the wildness, the drowning, the clawing released him, estranged him, so that he knew *Jules* could have been any name and any man and any plunging into her, arms, legs, thighs, mouths, bellies, hands, groping clutching failing fingers....Her mouth twisted so that she was not even pretty, but he shut his eyes, loving her, *yesJulesJulesysslyss*, and hours later rose from her enflamed, dry-mouthed, a blood-misty film across his eyes and clammy webs between his fingers, an animal padding barefoot across a carpeted room, flinching from the surprise of normal sounds outside: car doors slamming, children's voices.

Then he returned and lay beside her, beside a girl sleeping with her lips parted, her breath raspy, child-like, and though he tried to keep awake he must have fallen asleep at once, no more questions, no more Jules.

In the morning, shyness, the raw bleak air and the sound of gulls, Jules husbandly, the girl taking very long—fifteen, twenty minutes—in the bathroom while he waited half dressed, staring at his toes, the grime between his toes, trying to think: What should he do with her? It seemed to him that he had the right to demand something from her, the promise of her, he had the right even to threaten her....She must confess, must tell him everything, or he would not go any farther: he would refuse to drive her any farther. But he was shy, strangely shy, and their eyes had darted together in a shy fierce glance, both of them asking *Do you still...?* and afraid even of kissing, afraid of being rejected, the sky shone into the room through a window above the door and showed neutral, rather white-glaring day, not flattering them, blunt, matter-of-fact, vivid. Jules felt married to her, seeing her shrink back from him: not so certain of herself, really, and not that beautiful a girl, not at all times.

...let me drive you away, somewhere else.

Then it was husbandly of Jules to help unsnag some of her hair, caught in a zipper, and wifely of Dewalene to say he must have breakfast, there was a restaurant in the motel that would be fine for breakfast, she'd stopped there once years ago...he had to eat, he looked hungry. Jules laughed and joked that he always looked hungry; he'd looked like this, ravaged and hollow-stomached, all his life. And said nothing to her about that day's destination, which he gathered was somewhere to the north and the east, up into the mountains.

He had two eggs and toast and a side-order of pancakes, and coffee, and at first Dewalene shuddered, having no appetite, then she accepted some of his breakfast—picking at the scrambled eggs daintily, sitting close beside him in a booth facing the road—then let him call the waitress back and order a breakfast for her, because by now she was trembling with hunger and murmuring, I don't know what's wrong with me, I guess I'm not well yet...trying to laugh, saying Someone seems to be inside me, at times, a stranger pushing his way up inside me and through me....

Is that God?

...but Jules didn't ask her that. Instead he smiled at her eating part of his breakfast and said, *Let me be him, then*, but it was playful, light-toned. He was thinking that he did want her, he wanted her, yes, he wanted what she was and more: what he could transform her into. She was not nearly as beautiful as she was meant to be. He knew that. *Let me, let me!*...Her small sweet breathless cries, her lips rubbed bare of lipstick, the tense cords in her throat, the strong curve of her stomach, the way she was sitting close beside him in a booth in a noisy restaurant, with paper place-mats that were cartoon maps of the United States, coffee-stained from earlier customers—he was dizzy with the certainty of it, Jules at the center of the universe, he knew he was right, he was right.

Were you ever married?

Were you?

No.

No.

Were you almost married?

O yes!

Yes!

But Jules went one step farther and asked, *Who was he...?*

Dewalene stiffened.

Who?

Whoever it was.

He paid the check, an expensive breakfast—$4.21!—and when he went outside she was already in the car, a girl with blue-tinted glasses in a car that struck Jules as incredibly ugly. But you must get in, you must drive it. You must.

You must ask questions not to be asked.

tell me who he was and I
will never ask about him
will forgive—
never think about him or
envy him or
want to kill him or
strangle you with your hair

Bare ground, bare strident ridges of rock, foothills with brightly-colored rocks: a silvery rose, so lovely Jules found himself staring at it, into it, the sheer shimmering beauty of color, hypnotized. Dewalene was silent beside him. In the canyon hills were cascades of poplars and eucalyptus trees with their long, narrow leaves, the green/silver of their leaves, and large yellow daisies, and orange poppies, and weeds of purple and blue, dust-sprinkled, sun-baked, all silent. *What is this?*—Jules wanted to ask. *What is this, this world?*

It baffled him.

The girl beside him stared out at the wilderness, staring, her profile turned from him, the gravity of her body some-how apart from him, leaning toward the door as if she wanted it to open and release her. Jules saw a flight of birds and asked her what they were and she said, only glancing at them, Oh just quail or doves, and he felt the estrangement in her; the opposition. His own anger rose, prepared. He was always prepared. But he appeared not to notice her lethargy and talked to her about how he had come to love this part of the world, how he'd bought a car one spring just to drive out into the Mojave Desert and up into the San Bernardino Mountains and how it had transformed him—Jules, a boy from the city, city-bred, city-staggered, how he had been born in the country but had come to live in the city too young, and had been nearly destroyed by it. Dewalene nodded, listening or not quite listening. She was turned away from him, staring at the empty land. They were passing between the walls of a canyon, on a narrow rocky road, scrub pines on either side, and a blast of sunlight showed an intense almost painfully vivid wall of brown-pink, mauve-brown-pink, so beautiful that Jules stopped the car.

They sat there for a while, without speaking.

…then Dewalene said, not turning to him but reaching out to him, touching his arm, her fingers closing about his arm, Jules, you're going to have to let me go.…

Again he kept his anger down. He asked her what she meant…?

Because I have commitments to someone.

Permanent commitments?

No.

He glanced out, around at the slanted, fading light, the eerie rock walls that were so brutal, and almost as he stared the landscape shifted, became cruel, its beauty was no beauty he now valued, he wanted only Dewalene and *he wanted her*, he said ironically, *Then I get another chance at you, sometime?*

Dewalene took off her sunglasses and rubbed her nose and eyes, wearily. Jules had the sudden desire to snatch the glasses from her and break them in two, *You bitch, what are your secrets?—where are you going?—who is waiting for you?* But he said nothing. Evidently she wasn't going to answer him so he started the car again, it stalled, he started it again angrily, thinking it would be good, wonderful, if this car stalled up in the hills and he and Dewalene were stranded, *This damn car of yours*, he muttered, but finally he got it going again and his face glowed angrily with the shame of it, the struggle.

Dewalene checked the map. She told him it was only a short distance now—another fifty miles—and Jules made a sound that indicated All right, fine.

…Why are you angry, why do you hate me? Why do you want me to hate you? But she did not speak, she said none of this, and Jules drove faster than he should have driven, expecting to hear the car scrape against a rock, something shrieking as it was torn and mangled from beneath.

The afternoon was fading, light haloed Dewalene's hair, her head, Jules found himself thinking of the delirious halo of love, the perspiration-haze of love, and smiling grinning he wanted it, wanted it bitterly, but knew he was not going to get it. A god had eased into his body and filled it out, powerfully, demonically, but now the god had slipped away again and Jules could only remember, with lust, the bright-glistening struggle of love, his own choked cries of pleasure, muscle transformed into light, airy light, how he yearned for that Jules again!—the god-in-Jules again!— but he would not speak to her, he was not going to hear his own ironic defeated voice again, *Then I get another chance at you…?* Because he was thinking, he was forcing himself to think these ugly things, that maybe what he lusted for, was only the god-in-Jules and not this girl at all, maybe she was accidental to it, to him, and let her return to her friends, her protectors, let her sleep with whoever had the power to keep her.…Tears of anger stung his eyes. Tears. Dry-aching eyeballs blurred with tears, and not soothed by them, because they were a sign of his defeat and nothing else.…

Please don't drive so fast!—Dewalene said, frightened.

He slowed down.

Never would he mock her: never would he say *But aren't you in a hurry to get to him?*

He knew better than to say such flat defeated things. He had been her lover, after all. He was proud of himself and would not speak viciously to her, though he had flashes of strange visions—the Jaguar end-over-end down the rocky slope here, to crash five hundred feet below, Jules and Dewalene doll-like and helpless as they fell—no— ahead was a bridge, a swift-flowing river, why not drive the car into that?—but no, no, he was too sane, he did not want to die and did not really want her to die, after all she was so much in love with him. He hated himself saying gently, alarmed at the gentleness of his own voice:

…but I don't want to let you go.…

But you don't love me!—she cried.

Jules was hurt. He said, *Why do you say that?—you know that I—*

—you won't let me alone, you would never let me forget,

if we slept together the rest of our lives, in each other's arms, you would want to slip into my dreams and control them—you would want to own me and all the past I lived through and just want to forget—

Then forget it, forget it!—Jules wanted to say. But he knew she was right: his silence seemed part of a formal, familiar argument, as if the two of them had already been married for a long time, and now he must be silent, hurt and angry and silent, to force her to hear again her own words, to punish her with her words.

Say something to me, she pleaded.

Jules shrugged his shoulders. *What can I say?*

—if you want to ask me about—

No, said Jules sadly, *not at all.*

—I was just a witness to—

No.

Below was the Black Fox River, Jules saw a sign stuck crooked at the edge of the road; below the road a rocky incline, dropping to the river and out of the levelling rays of the sun, which was setting early, it seemed to Jules, everything was stark and too clear in the sunlight and then abruptly, horribly shadowed where the sunlight no longer reached....*The Black Fox River*, he said, and Dewalene said, dully and mechanically, yes, according to the map that was right, that was right.

He drove along the river for a few miles, high above it, slowing because of the sharp, hair-pin turns, without protective barriers and no warning except rusted, battered old signs: DANGER.

His heart had heaved itself against her. Lifting, heaving. He had not cared then in what patches, in what unreadable hieroglyphics the sweat of other men had dried on her body, he hadn't cared who had kissed her face into that shape, and who she imagined inside her—whom she clutched at, loving, calling him *Jules*— All the names were one, all men were one, and Jules had become them all. He had known it. That was why he wanted her, he wanted what she was and could become, and he wanted what he himself could become—lifted so high by her, and then lying free of the poison of his own feverish brain, everything impure pumped out of him, drained away, so that he was pure and nameless, lying in her arms. He knew all this, but he said nothing. Let her leave him, let her go!— he knew she would regret it. And he would regret it too.

...thinking about?

About getting out of here before it's dark.

You can leave me off at the turn-off, she said. *You don't have to stay with me until they pick me up.*

I didn't think you would want me to stay, Jules said politely.

No, it's only an hour, no, forty-five minutes, I can wait, Dewalene said.

They passed a caretaker's cabin, which looked deserted. The road was lifting, rising into the foothills. Dewalene said, *There, up ahead*, and at first Jules saw nothing but pine trees and then he saw a clearing, another cabin, an old campfire site and debris scattered thinly around it...at the edge of the road a deer paused, frightened, and then bounded in front of the car and out of sight into the woods. *Stop here*, Dewalene said.

Here?

A road goes off to the left, back there, back that way, Dewalene said. She knelt on the seat and reached into the back, and Jules sat there numbly, staring at the cabin— made of real logs—and the trail that led back from the road and the curiously blue, hard blue sky, which had become slightly filmy now, with long thin smoky clouds of a bluish-orange hue.

You've been here before…?

Just once before.

What about the car?

Keep it.

…keep it?

She laughed and brushed her hair out of her eyes. Now she was excited, eager. She stared at Jules. She said, *You're right to let me go, we'll arrange to meet again…keep the car, or give it back to me when we meet…In a few weeks….*

After the trial is over, Jules said, not returning her smile.

Yes.

Were you subpoenaed?

She looked past him. He saw her face go stubborn, hard.

Which side…? said Jules.

Dewalene shook her head. She was just a witness, she said softly, only a witness, only one of many witnesses, what did it matter…? And things that had happened in her presence had not happened in Jules' presence. And people who had met through her and in her, people who had come together in her, all those people, Jules could not know them and could not remember them, just as she could not remember them, not clearly, why didn't he love her, why was he letting her go?...something had happened to her that had terrified her, she'd run away from it, she'd made a mistake to run away from it, and now *Jules hears her faint perplexed voice*

He drove back, toward the river.

But a mile or two of the car's slow dream-like dipping and he was stricken in the chest, the throat, he felt the tears sting at the corners of his eyes, he thought *No, it's a mistake, your mind is making you do the wrong thing.* As, one time when he'd first come out here, and was in a lavatory somewhere, a little drunk, fearful of vomiting, a man had hesitantly approached him and waited until Jules noticed him and had stared, stared intently into Jules' narrowed eyes, and Jules had felt a rising maniacal rage in him, If you touch me I'll kill you, and his mind had cunningly directed even the expression of his face so that, yes, the man would be led to touch him—and how anguished, how desperate he had been!—just the touch of his shaking fingers releasing in Jules a delight of viciousness, a rage that fanned over his brain, like flames, really flame-like, rippling into every part of his body—

After the first blow and the first leap of blood, after Jules' silent attack, the man falling away and clutching at the sink, his fingers failing, his head striking the dirty tiled wall, Jules knew it was a mistake, his mind was making him do evil, he didn't really want to be pounding with his fists, grunting, at some stranger's body, but— *Why so barbarous, why shouting No, no! Always no!* He had to run out of that stinking place and into the dizzying chilly air of the mountains, out of the meek-eyed stranger's bleeding face to his own face mashed, nose broken and gushing blood, and back there in the clearing Dewalene lying, dead— But no, no, he saw that it was only a tarpaulin of some kind, which he hadn't noticed before. He got out of the car. *Dewalene?* It was very quiet. He walked around, he looked in the cabin—nothing to see—and observed the scattered tin cans and beer cans and the old rotted canvas—

With his foot he lifted the canvas a little—nothing under it—dried-out flattened-down grass, dead.

I was just a witness.

So he got back in the car and turned it around again, just as he'd turned it around before, the same maneuver, the same anxiety that he not back into one of the trees, three separate awkward maneuvers it took him to turn that damn car around, except this time the girl was not watching him and he had not the terror, the sick dissolving terror, of knowing how she watched him calmly and how he was going to drive away while she still watched him, calmly, and he would even wave to her and she would even wave back....

Before dark, just before dark—and he was back at the paved road, a two-lane road running along the Black Fox River, so now he was safe, he was headed back down. He turned the lights on—fumbling for the knob—and up ahead he saw another vehicle, he saw its red tail lights— His first instinct was fear, but no, no, his real emotion was relief, that someone else was driving down from the mountains and he might be able to follow, keeping the tail lights in view....Coming around a curve he saw a motorcyclist ahead, the man's white helmet glowing, glaring in the headlights, for now it was suddenly dark: it had happened suddenly. The motorcyclist was driving slowly, maybe five miles an hour, and Jules would have to pass him. He saw that it was a highway patrolman—a man in a uniform— and Jules passed him carefully, in no hurry, *how he feared the police!* thinking suddenly that he did not own the car and could not explain it and could not explain himself *oh Christ just let me get by him*...but the patrolman stared at him, and made that dread motion with his gloved hand that meant *Pull over, pull over ahead....*

Jules could not believe it.

His breath went ragged, in one instant. This could not be happening. It could not. It could not be happening. Yet he saw very clearly the man's raised hand, he saw the man move gracefully on the motorcycle, speeding up to overtake Jules....

He wondered: Should he drive out of here?

He wondered: Was there a gun somewhere...?

But quietly, sanely, he braked to a stop at once, he knew better than to fight, he had done nothing wrong, had broken no laws, he was innocent and had no reason to feel so guilty, so sickly panicked...but the patrolman motioned him ahead, up ahead, he should drive along....The man followed him, out in the other lane, just beyond Jules' left rear fender. Jules was sweating freely, but his mind directed him well enough: Do what you're instructed to do, keep your foot steady on the accelerator, *oh my God now what?* there must be some simple explanation for this, his mind gave a leap and made him grin, crazy with the thought *Oh, the bastard is selling raffle tickets, maybe*, and Jules composed his face alert and sane and uncalculating as the patrolman now drove up alongside him and indicated he should pull over. Over to the side. Over here. He flagged Jules across to the other lane.

Jules put on the hand-brake and looked over and down, down to the river.

He thought it was strange, that the patrolman should have him park here.

O.K., said the officer, *get out.*

Jules got out. He saw, parked a hundred yards away, a car with its lights out; it was parked in the middle of the road. *No sudden movements*, said the patrolman, though Jules had made no sudden movements, not even to get his wallet out of his back pocket. He was too nervous to think *why is this happening?* or to look down the drop-off to the river, the rocky-jutting sheer drop, no, he wasn't looking down there but at the patrolman's California-tanned face. The man was about Jules' age, husky, broad-shouldered in his black leather jacket with its many buckles and flaps and its straight proud glinting zipper. He was telling Jules what the law was in this state about moving vehicles, something about after-dark driving and how both tail lights must be in good working order, and Jules stared at him, nodding dully, not comprehending....

The man smiled at him, a small mean cheerless smile. He asked Jules where he was heading so fast...? Jules replied that he had not been speeding; he had been driving only about twenty-five miles an hour. The man nodded, as if leading him on. Twenty-five miles an hour was it, well then what was the hurry?—around these curves, without any guard rails, most motorists drive slower than that. You must be from out-of-state, he said, glancing behind Jules at the other car. You must not know our laws.

Jules said nothing.

You must not know our laws, the patrolman repeated.

Shivering, Jules glanced over his shoulder—yes, there was a car parked down the road—but why, why parked there, why its headlights out—he was aware of the noise of the river and the patrolman's taunting-intimate voice, not a familiar voice but one which seemed to know Jules well, saying now *Do you know our laws about interfering in private domestic disagreements?* and when Jules didn't answer, gone cold and sullen, he said something about the penal code, the penalties exacted under California law for conveying parties out of the county they are enjoined not to leave, didn't Jules know about that?—and what about driving a car not his own, with no access to the registration papers, no way of proving whose car it was or whether it was a stolen car or *it was a rotted canvas, a tarpaulin lying on the flattened-down dead weeds* a car involved in a crime, a car used for an escape, a car belonging to someone very dangerous...and was Jules aware of this?

The patrolman spoke in a rapid taunting manner, as if going down a list of memorized items, stray grins and twitches in his cheeks meant to inform Jules that *this cannot be serious, no* but Jules could not respond with a smile, no, and when a voice sounded from the other car—a faint shout—he had not the strength to turn that way, to look.

Yes all right *compensation* muttered the patrolman, whose jaw shifted from side to side, disappointed that this should come to an end, we're going to compensate for your inconvenience, it's a very stiff penal code but aimed to rehabilitate rather than punish, we just confiscate the car and no questions asked on either side....*Here you are, for your inconvenience and for the car*, the man said, taking from his pocket an envelope and holding it out to Jules.

Jules took it.

If you don't trust us, look inside; count it.

What is it? said Jules. *What—*

Count it, you bastard!

Jules opened the envelope, which was not sealed, and extracted some bills—stiff new bills, which stuck together— but his head rang, he couldn't see the numbers on the bills, and the patrolman was already telling him to move out of the way, to get walking in that direction—*which? where?—what are you going to do?*

Not what you deserve, the man said.

Jules backed away.

At the other car they opened a door for him and he

climbed in. The back seat was empty except for someone's raincoat, a lightweight coat carelessly folded. In the front seat, not looking at Jules, as if not really aware of him, were two men he didn't recognize; the driver immediately started the car, turned on the headlights—the man in the policeman's outfit did not raise his gloved hand, or smile, but stared at them, standing by the gleaming grill-work of the Jaguar—and made a U-turn, driving off onto the shoulder of the road, bouncing on the bumpy ground, and Jules' head rattled with the *What was it, who was he, which one of them was I*—and they let him out early that morning on Highway 395, so that he could get a ride to the nearest town—Alturas—from there, since it was close to Reno, Nevada.

...where he finally counted it, three thousand in one-hundred-dollar bills, and stuffed them in his pocket and

Is she dead?

Dead, they muttered, dead, dead or living, what's that? —what year is it, back there?

Is she alive?—back there?

Oh everybody's alive, back there, they told him, and Jules blinked the stinging out of his eyes, the fizzing, wondering if he would soar to the surface of his pain as he had the other time in Ventura County General Hospital but no, if he could remember that other time this time could not be it, he could not even sleep this time because of all the noise, Jules himself crying *What do you mean?—don't you care?—doesn't it mean anything, life or death?*

They're all dead, back there.

No, alive.

But is she alive?—is *she*?

The Chief of Medicine, a man with a pallid, creased face, leaned over Jules and put one big cool protective hand against Jules' feverish forehead, the palm of his hand firm, solid, saying over his shoulder *This one is too weak to talk, is he in shock...?*

No, Jules cried, *I'm awake, I'm alive* and then his mind leaped *Except once I turned over something on my plate and it had a fishskin soft and black speckled like a snake and I gagged and I thought Snakes snakes we would eat them too if we had to, we'd eat anything, oh Christ anything anything.*

No sin in that, where is the sin? The Chief of Medicine held Jules' head, fatherly but formal, remote, saying to someone *This one isn't ready for me—he's going to tear out the tubes and make a mess—*

He felt a needle sink into his arm, his upper arm where there had been muscle he remembered but now he could not remember: Jules? Dewalene? Without their bodies were they lovers?—without two bodies could they love? But beneath the torn tarpaulin there had been nothing. He had lifted it carefully with one foot: nothing. The clearing had been empty. The sky empty. Nothing. From the mountains shadows, the faint whirring of a helicopter, shadowy confused rustlings of tree boughs, creatures in the woods, a startled deer leaping out in front of the car, Dewalene closing her eyes *I was only a witness...don't you*

love me? Jules had found no solution to his life in Reno,
Nevada, though he spent much of the money getting drunk
and throwing up on tiled floors or out in the street, where
cars careened past honking horns at him or at the blazing
night sky or at the young girls hitch-hiking right in the city,
in blue jeans cut off at the thigh, tossing their long scissors-
cut hair at him too young for him, too young and evil. No,
no solution. Long ago he had argued himself into thinking
that he could not be blamed, not for anything that happened to him or anything he caused to happen, not Jules,
not Jules in his innocence, he could not be blamed for the
consequences of his life, *he was not a real person*—the
terrible secret of his soul, that he somehow did not believe
he was real!—but in Reno or whatever it was he got to,
unshaven and hollow-eyed and sick, deathly sick, sick as if
he had witnessed her death, as if he had been trapped in
that car pushed down into the river, end-over-end into the
river, down the slope of the rock-studded bank and into
the river, he could see his own hair lifting ghastly from his
head and his eyes open, drowned, blank, as he sat trapped
behind the wheel unmoving and Dewalene beside him
with her long hair lifting, waving wildly in that fast-moving
stream, he heard the sirens screaming night after night in
Reno and wondered: Was it the end of the world? Fires,
an earthquake, bombs? Or just another night in Reno? —
and nothing happened, not even when he staggered into
someone in a lavatory and the man shoved him brutally
away, the man alertly vicious as Jules himself had been
months before, but not as eager to strike out as Jules had

been—only the shoving-back against the wall, the thump of Jules' back and shoulders against the wall—and a gang of prowling kids, white boys, hadn't bothered him though he had on his person more than $2000 at that time; though looking so strung-out, so wretched, that they could not have guessed.

He walked out of a city, out into the desert, where the unrottable glass and tin cans and other metallic debris lay glinting year after year, immortal, thinking that his own body would take a long time to rot, on this hard-packed sandy earth, so dry, so unhuman. He lay flat: thinking it was like lying flat against a well, a vast architectural facade he could not see, could not imagine, like a lizard clinging to the side of an immense wall on an immense structure given a name in some language *A man burning slowly in the sun, the process of his burning speeded up, all his ages crammed into one age: one final date-of-death* but it wasn't very sunny or very warm, strangely like winter, a dull-glowing sun and layers of cloud, the slow-shivering gray-ness, gusts of indifferent chill wind, the sound of small whirl-winds that concentrated into the sound of jet-planes high overhead, passing high above him, at such speed and at such altitude that the roar encompassed every horizon, then faded and faded into the panic of vomiting, the quick need to turn his head or it would choke him gag him *Which one of them was I? What did I do to her?* And suddenly he did not mind. He did not mind. Only losing her, backing the car around with that caution not even in his own nature, his own personality, leaving her, losing her: his one mistake. But his own life, his own going-into-craziness, his own death, really he did not mind any of it because he could no longer believe in it, he was too lonely, he existed out here in the desert where there were only two dimensions.

Calmed by the sedative he surveyed the bed and realized why he was so unhappy: his heels went an inch or more beyond the edge of the mattress, his toes were pressed down by the heavy blanket. They asked him how he felt, he was too cunning to reply, they drew nearer and observed that his eye-muscles moved therefore no injury to the brain, and cunning themselves they complimented him on his color, not parchment-color now, the dehydration no danger now and cunning they asked him *Would he sign a release?* And Jules knew the answer must be *Yes.* He knew that. Someone must have instructed him, someone he could not recall, the answer must be yes, the answer to all questions yes, *Yes.* But he lay silent, stubborn in his mourning. *Yes* was the answer he must give, to whatever was or wasn't under the tarpaulin or crashing down the cliff to the Black Fox River, yes to his own blood drained out of him dripping into sterilized bottles to be stored in a refrigerated room *O.K., this one's O.K. —we got the Wassermann back from the lab this morning*, yes to his guts yanked out of him by strangers wearing flesh-colored skin-tight rubber gloves, you must say yes in the end, you should have been murmuring yes all along, wisely a nurse had comforted him the night before while poking around for a vein *Well you loved her for a while, she lived for a while, you'd better sign the release* and Jules knew it was yes, yes, a windstorm had howled *Yes* over him one day or night out there, and the thunderous Pacific outside their motel room had aided them in their love crying *Yes yes* and his father at supper threatening to push in his smirky face had whispered *Yes* to him beneath all that shouting and Jules had known it, had known it, but thick and dense in him, stubborn, almost malicious in mourning, a kind of clot of a soul would not speak, lay mute, dehydrated of emotion but stubborn with the memory of it *I still love her and I still want her*

One of them kicked the bed. *We hear that!—we hear every word!*

But Jules kept it

and the bed was kicked again, violently, kicked so that it skidded a few inches out into the aisle *Go back then, you bastard*

The sedative was wearing off. He could not locate where the pain first began but suddenly it fizzed everywhere, light and wild, like the stinging of insects so rapid and delicate that pain itself was slow to coalesce, and visions popped beneath his closed eyelids, dry, abrasive, on the very surface of his eyeballs: he saw the girl there, across the two-storey drop, he saw a man lower himself upon her and the two of them struggling, come to desperate horrible life in their struggle while he stared through the binoculars *oh Christ* and coldly sweating he saw himself bent over someone, a body, his naked back gleaming with sweat *Yes yes* that was Jules, and how maddened he was with it, pumping love into another squirming body, the skin raw, chafed, the flesh beneath the girl's small breasts slightly reddened, heat-prickled but he cannot stop *He cannot stop* and now someone paws at him, yearning for him, but he is too strong and shoves the man away and feels the splatter of blood on his fist and helplessly he clambers on top of someone, he forces someone's knees apart sobbing because he cannot stop he cannot stop his sister screams for him to stop, to get away, it is his own sister *But I never did this* and back again he lies in his own bed, his own room, his heart pumping pounding stiffening swelling in his eyeballs swooning back in his head with lust with the craziness of lust *But I never crawled in her room and* he seizes her by the ankles by her thin threshing legs and *Christ help me to stop help me* but the bed has been kicked cruelly off into the night, into Jules' delirious sleep, it spins helplessly now as if borne along on a black-flowing river *It cannot stop* and he sees his sister's face bruised and senseless beneath him and whispers to her *No not even now I can't stop even now* and finally it is a woman with his mother's face but no body he ever remembered but maybe he did remember it, standing before a mirror, his mother as a girl and so young! so young! and not seeing him she stares into the mirror into the future *Everything is there, waiting* while Jules squirms with his lust, gone mad with his lust, the universe crammed into his body and squeezing him out of shape, go back you bastard, back you go, back you go and all over again and again the strong healthy bland pretty face and the blue eyes not seeing him where he crouched, the gaze-upon-gaze of her staring, and her face suddenly expanding before him like a sky fitted curving over the earth, and again the immense warm flesh of her body, gigantic now, mountainous in his hot-staring eyes, oh he is terrified of this woman and yet he must enter her, every pore of his body craves to enter her, *to enter her*, the face is too enormous now to be seen and it falls away and the other faces fall away, rearing back into night, none of them have faces now, none of them know him, he knows none of them, but borne along wildly on that flood he shrivels to a pinpoint of light deep inside this woman, inside her womb, a pinpoint of light that shudders and falters but does not go out—